My Stupid Intentions

BERNARDO ZANNONI

Translated from the Italian by Alex Andriesse

 New York Review Books New York

This is a New York Review Book
published by The New York Review of Books
207 East 32nd Street, New York, NY 10016
www.nyrb.com

Originally published in the Italian language as *I miei stupidi intenti*.

This book was translated, in part, thanks to a grant awarded by the Italian
Ministry of Foreign Affairs and International Cooperation.

Library of Congress Cataloging-in-Publication Data
Names: Zannoni, Bernardo, 1995– author. | Andriesse, Alex, translator.
Title: My stupid intentions / Bernardo Zannoni; translated by Alex Andriesse.
Other titles: Miei stupidi intenti. English
Description: New York: New York Review Books, [2023]
Identifiers: LCCN 2022020173 (print) | LCCN 2022020174 (ebook) |
  ISBN 9781681377285 (paperback) | ISBN 9781681377292 (ebook)
Subjects: LCGFT: Animal fiction. | Novels.
Classification: LCC PQ4926.A368 M5413 2023 (print) |
  LCC PQ4926.A368 (ebook) | DDC 853/.92—dc23/eng/20220429
LC record available at https://lccn.loc.gov/2022020173
LC ebook record available at https://lccn.loc.gov/2022020174

ISBN 978-1-68137-728-5
Available as an electronic book; ISBN 978-1-68137-729-2

Printed in the United States of America on acid-free paper.

10 9 8 7 6 5 4 3 2 1

1

Winter, Our Mother

MY FATHER DIED because he was a thief. He stole three times from the Fields of Zò, and on the fourth the man caught him. He shot him in the belly, tore the chicken from his mouth, and tied him to a fence post as a warning. He left his partner with six kits on her plate, in the middle of winter, with the snow already on the ground.

Through the blizzarding nights, all lumped together in the same big bed, we watched as our mother despaired in the kitchen, in the half light of the lamp under the den's low ceiling.

"Damn it, Davis, damn it!" she cried. "Now what am I supposed to do? You stupid marten!"

We watched her and didn't make a sound, huddled close against the cold. On my right was my brother Leroy and on my left Joshua, whom I never got to know. He must have died not long after he was born, perhaps crushed by our mother when she lay down for a nap.

"You scoundrel!" she cried. "And now who's going to raise these orphans?"

In those early days life was a beautiful feeling. Beneath the covers, breathing nice and easy, you drifted off into the most vivid sleep. You were fragile and strong, hidden from the world and waiting to venture out into it.

"Who's going to raise them? Who's going to raise them?" our mother said. Then she would come over to the bed and lie down, offering us her belly. The moment I sensed it, I clung to it with all my strength. Instantly my siblings started scrapping for space. Leroy, the biggest, went barreling in, while the girls, Cara and Louise, teamed up. Otis, the youngest, was often the odd one out.

"Who's going to raise them? Who's going to raise them?" our mother said. Every now and then I would feel her wince in pain, when one or another of us bit down too hard. Joshua was sticking out from beneath her fur, not moving.

At night she'd leave us to go looking for food and during the day grab a few hours' sleep. Once in a while, if she found something of value, she'd go out in broad daylight to trade for food with Solomon the lender. She was gaunt and her belly hung down on the ground. Dragging it over the snow must have chilled her to the bone.

"Pipe down, kits," she'd say, whenever we woke her. And she went on saying it every waking hour.

"Pipe down, pipe down."

We were beginning to speak. And to range about. One morning Leroy fell out of bed, crawled all around it, and couldn't manage to climb back up. He would have died from the cold if our mother hadn't come home. Before setting him back onto the bed I remember she hesitated a few moments, which I couldn't comprehend. Though if one of us had been in her place, we might well have left him where he was. Leroy was the biggest and the strongest of us.

It snowed and snowed, sometimes for days on end. On one occasion the entrance to the den was blocked up, and our mother spent hours trying to dig a tunnel out.

"Pipe down, pipe down!" she shouted, whenever any of us complained we were hungry.

Every now and then I'd see her sitting in the kitchen staring into the void. She'd smooth her whiskers and sigh, not saying a word but as if she were talking with someone. Whenever she behaved this way, I'd linger and look. I sensed she wasn't well, that something wasn't right, and this frightened me. But before I knew it my eyes had closed, and when I opened them again she was gone.

"Don't get sick, I can't afford the doctor," she told us once, after we'd started romping around the den. Her warning wasn't lost on any of us, and indeed we never even ventured near the window, let alone outside. But Otis was the only one who never climbed out of bed, and the girls used to tease him.

"You're such a runt, Otis, you'd break your neck."

When Leroy started touching everything around the place, I mimicked him. We didn't talk much. He would pick something up, look at it, then put it back, and I'd do the same. I studied whatever I had between my paws in a hurry, though, because my brother's attention was quickly on to something else and I didn't want to fall behind.

Our mother steered clear of us if she were on her way somewhere. As far as she was concerned we weren't even in the room. When she suckled we all jumped on the bed, where Otis, luckily for him, had already had a few moments to feed.

"You're hurting me," she'd murmur in irritation whenever one of us got carried away. Usually that was enough to calm us down, but sometimes she'd curse and swipe at us with a paw, claws in.

We were almost always hungry, and cold too. Some days we hardly got out of bed and wrestled with our stomach cramps beneath the covers, nestled close. One time Leroy nudged me awake.

"Are you cold?" he said.

"I'm hungry."

"Me too. We could eat Otis. He's small, and weak."

I never thought for a moment it might be a joke. With my tongue I touched the little teeth growing from my gums and said nothing.

"So?"

"Maybe I'm more cold than I am hungry."

Our mother came back into the den before he could respond. Somehow I thought I might have offended him with my cowardice, and for a while, even after I'd eaten, I couldn't get to sleep. That was the day I began to comprehend there was a slight, horrible difference between me and Leroy: He was more of an animal than I was. To think that he also realized this was very upsetting. But neither of us ate Otis. Nor did Leroy eat me.

One night our mother came home with a very peculiar object. She set it on the table and gave us a warning.

"Don't touch it. This thing will keep us in food for a while."

We waited for her to fall asleep before going to see what it was.

"It's a lady's jewel," said Cara. "One of man's little treasures."

It was a roundish trinket that shone green and lovely in the light. Lying there on the table, it seemed to speak to each of us in secret. Leroy nudged and touched it with his paw.

"It's cold," he said. "Like the air outside."

I wanted to touch it too. But our mother had been clear, and I was afraid she'd wake up. The thought of disobeying her gave rise to horrible things in my imagination, especially since back then I'd never seen the consequences. Louise leapt onto the table, picked it up, studied it innocently, and slipped it over her paw like a bracelet.

"Don't, Louise! No, she doesn't want us to," Cara hissed.

"I'm the most beautiful of all," said Louise, ignoring her sister.

"It isn't true!"

Cara jumped on the table and lunged at Louise.

"Mama doesn't want us to!"

She struggled to pull the trinket off her paw, but Louise thrashed and bit her.

"Stop that! Leave me alone!"

It didn't take Leroy and me long to see what was coming. In the blink of an eye, we slipped off the table into the far corner of the room.

"It's not yours!"

"Leave me alone!"

And it fell, shattering into four pieces with a dry-sounding crack. From the depths of the bed, our mother sat witnessing it all. The two sisters remained frozen to the spot as she climbed down and came to see what was left of the trinket. She picked up the pieces and stared at them.

"Mama . . ." Cara murmured.

She was quick and precise. With one paw she smacked our sister's snout and knocked her off the table. Louise flinched and began to shake but didn't say a word. My heart pounded. Leroy, feeling something soft on his fur, pulled at it to see what it was.

While Cara began to cry, we stared at that strange white-and-red lump, as it slowly dawned on us it was a chunk of her eyeball. Our sister held her head with one paw, stifling the pain as the blood mottled her face. Leroy let the eye fall to the ground. For a moment I had thought he might eat it.

Our mother threw the shards on the table by Louise, who'd gathered all her limbs around her like a fortress, to ward off blows.

"Scum," she said, without looking at any of us, then went out into the freezing night.

I heard her come in the next morning. She shuffled into the kitchen and stared into the void. In the sunlight she looked skinnier than ever. I climbed out of bed in silence while the others were still asleep.

"Mama?"

She turned slowly around. Perhaps she'd heard me coming. She seemed to look right through me.

"Do you feel bad about Papa?" I asked.

She didn't answer. She never did.

2

The Crow, the Nest

AT THE TAIL END OF SPRING, we ventured out of the den. The wind was cool and still biting, tousling your fur. I remember the moment I first stuck my nose outside—the explosion of odors and perfumes, which drove my senses to distraction. We lived under a rock very near two trees. In the morning it was in the shade, and at dusk the setting sun caressed the ground. Our mother told us only four things.

"To the right and behind you is the forest. To the left the Three Streams. Straight ahead are the Fields of Zò. Stay out of trouble."

She wouldn't let us go with her. If any of us followed, she would notice immediately and chase us away. This made Leroy furious. He began keeping to himself and wandering off on his own.

Since Otis could never stay outside for long, and Cara, now blind in one eye, had lost all appetite for play, I spent much of my time with Louise. We chased each other around.

"You can't catch me, Archy."

She always got away. She'd slink into the bushes and make herself invisible. But if I caught her we'd play-fight, giving each other sharp little nips.

We roamed around together, never straying too far from the den.

We had no neighbors apart from a family of hedgehogs away to the east. We'd only once caught a glimpse of them, scuttling back into their den. They lived in the trunk of a dead tree.

"Am I beautiful, Archy?"

Louise was always asking me this. Especially when we weren't on the move and simply sitting there in silence. I said yes.

"How beautiful?"

"Very beautiful."

"More beautiful than Cara?"

"Yes."

"Even than Mama?"

"Yes."

She would smooth her fur and stare off into the distance. Eventually I started to believe what I'd said. Perhaps it was on account of my instincts, or else by telling her so many times she was beautiful, that I ended up telling myself the same thing. But the fact is that, little by little, Louise went from being a sister to being an irresistible mystery.

"Am I beautiful, Archy?"

"As beautiful as can be."

"Thank you."

How I wished that, after she was finished smoothing her hair, her distant gaze would fix on me. When we chased after each other, I'd track her by her scent, and as we wrestled I'd nuzzle up against her, trading bite for bite.

In bed, leaning against Leroy's coarse back, I'd ask myself what this change meant. I'd think about why she could be so impetuous when I was with her, and also so bland and distant, until I drifted off to sleep.

*

Spring made everyone feel better. Our mother brought home food more often, and hunger no longer tormented us. Sometimes she came with little mice, sometimes with berries or fruit. She no longer looked so skinny, and her coat had again begun to shine.

"Pipe down," she'd still say, whenever we disturbed her.

As the days went by, we grew and grew; the features of our faces were becoming more distinct, one of us had lost his first milk teeth, and our coats were taking on color. While most of us marveled at our development, for one of us things took a different turn. Our brother Otis remained stunted, with paws that couldn't hold him up. He was scarcely able to climb onto the bed and could not get down on his own. No one paid him any mind, he existed not to be there, in the shadow of our lives. During meals we all stared at his plate.

"I'm going to die because I'm not growing," he said one evening at dinner.

All of us stopped eating for a moment, even our mother.

"Who told you that?" she said.

"No one. I just know. You haven't raised me, Mama." Two tears trickled down his gaunt snout.

"It's true," she said. Then she went back to eating again, and so did we. But no one took his plate.

One day Leroy came home with a crow. He'd hunted him down near the streams, as he'd been trying to do for weeks. The crow was beautiful, missing a wing, his feathers torn apart by bites and his beak hanging open. Our brother walked past us without a word and went

inside. He sat at the table, hunched over his prey. He was still breathing hard with his muscles tensed, his mouth bloody, his eyes the
watchful eyes of the hunter. He sat there and waited, not responding
to our questions, not letting us anywhere near the bird.

Perhaps because we had nothing to do, or perhaps because what
had happened was so extraordinary, we too just sat there and waited,
at a safe distance.

I remember that scene as a beautiful thing. All of us scattered
around the den staring at Leroy and the crow, who was as motionless
as the marten hunched over him, staring straight ahead.

Our mother came home after sunset with some berries to eat.
When she saw him—she was scarcely through the door—she
stopped in her tracks. The two of them stared at each other and did
not say a word.

"What's this?" she said.

"Dinner."

Our mother set the berries on the table.

"Your dinner, you mean."

Then she took the crow, ripped off his head, and started
cooking.

Watching Leroy eat that piece of meat shook me to the core. But
I felt something different from the envy of the others. I was trying
to work out what made my brother strong, stronger than I was. I felt
stupid. In bed his back looked as big as a mountain, and I kept
dreaming that I was being hunted like prey.

Our mother began taking Leroy with her. They rose early, and
I would watch them go out after a light breakfast, as quiet as could

be. They didn't say a word; they ate a bite and drank their water in silence. Together they came home with more food, and soon all of us began to eat more often. Once in a while they bought things from Solomon the lender, if they came across things of value on the hunt. Solomon marked all the items he sold with a little splash of color, or at least that's how it seemed to me.

Watching Leroy becoming an adult made me restless inside. Soon I too began to seek out solitude, wanting to prove myself. Louise didn't understand.

"Where are you going, Archy?"

"To the Three Streams."

"Why?"

I slipped away without further explanation, and she didn't try to follow me. It pained me to ignore her, but my anguish was stronger than my desire to be in her company.

The first few times I went to the Three Streams I hid in a bush and waited. A few birds flew above the trees overhead. Along the banks I saw nutria and, once, a badger.

Day after day my sense of anticipation increased, even when the dark had already grown thick around me. My mother never said a word when I came home late: I wanted so badly to be bringing something back.

Cara, with her single eye, was always sitting at the window. As I trotted home I could see the sharp shape of her silhouette pointed at the night, lost in unhappy thoughts.

I found a robins' nest at the top of a dying oak on which the sun scarcely shone. When I first saw it, I thought it was abandoned. The next day I watched while a mother bird soared in circles, landing only once she was certain there was no one around. After her came the father, then they both left together, going their separate ways. They returned and flew away again several times.

At home in bed I tossed and turned, trapped in a net, and woke up feeling I hadn't slept a wink. I crept out of the den, careful not to make a sound, shortly after our mother and Leroy left. The sky bathed the forest in a misty rain that stirred the air. It made no sound on the leaves, but it wasn't long before my coat was drenched. I made my way swiftly through the trees, looking neither right nor left, my heart urging me on toward the oak while I anxiously, recklessly sought the sight of its branches.

The nest was there, in the shadows. The two birds, curled up together to make a roof against the rain, appeared to be asleep. I concealed myself beneath them and settled in to wait. After a while I heard them talking. The rain was too light to cover their whispers and I could follow every topic they discussed. The female kept an ear out more than the male did, and when she got worried she went looking for him. I thought she'd spotted me, and my stomach turned to ice. I stayed stock-still, holding my breath, trying to work out if it were true, if I'd already let myself be discovered. At last he batted his wings and came flying his short way back to her, not saying another word. Then they seemed to go to sleep again.

I waited a while longer. Trying not to make a sound, I swatted a spider attempting to climb on my head, and cast my eyes upward. I wasn't thinking about anything; my whole self was concentrated on the image in front of me, the dark cocoon at the top of the dead branches, the two birds together. I was a motionless part of the world around me, more like a tree than an animal, perfectly fixed in its place, waiting.

The rain stopped. The birds shivered, shaking their little heads. She spoke to him again; he batted his wings to dry them. They touched lovingly, pinching each other with their beaks, and he flew away.

She shook off her feathers, hopped to the edge of the nest, and circled the tree one, two, three times. I held my breath as she passed swiftly overhead. After she'd finished the third circle, she too flew off into the distance.

Right away I sprung up and was at the foot of the oak. I jumped and anchored myself to the wood, pulling myself upward, holding on with my claws. With every leap skyward the earth moved farther away, my paws stayed fastened to the bark, and I proceeded rapidly, my fur bristling. When I arrived at the top of the trunk, I darted down a curved branch, then up again along a gaunt, contorted arm. I had no awareness of my fatigue or my low and steady breathing, much less the pain in my claws from scrabbling on the wood; I was nothing more than what I was seeing and doing, a spirit rooted in its deepest animal instinct.

Crack.

I stopped. The half of the branch I was standing on swayed, and I swayed with it. Rocked gently, filled with a horrible queasy feeling, I strained my eyes to pick out the nest.

And there it was, made of woven straw. From the ground I hadn't been able to see it clearly. My footing was no longer firm, and a little chill ran down my spine. With every wobbly step, I lost my balance, but I went on to the end, then stretched myself out toward the next branch. I grabbed on to it with my front paws, then leapt with the back ones. At the far end of this last pendent bridge was the nest. I took no notice of the splendid vista up there—that glimpse of the world that only those with wings can enjoy; even now, I regret it. Instead I looked into the two birds' nest, and saw—marvel of marvels—three bluish eggs.

I contemplated them for a long moment, still catching my breath. My eyes shone with pleasure, and for the first time a thought occurred to me: what it would be like going home to my mother.

I picked up one of the eggs and looked at it all over. It was warm. Leroy had his crow and I my three robin eggs. I was an adult.

Crack.

I did not sway, I plummeted straight down. When I realized what was happening, I was still holding the egg out in front of me. I let go of it, thrashed and flailed, looking left and right, but none of this did me any good.

My back smacked against one branch, then another, snapping it in two, and I continued my freefall, turning over on my legs, so that they ended up literally crushed into the ground.

I yelped in pain and sensed, on my tongue, the acrid taste of blood. My stomach contracted and churned laboriously, making me cough and cough as I tried to catch my breath, my eyes full of tears. Immediately fear urged me to get up and run away, but after two short steps I fell again. A sharp pain in my right leg kept me from going any farther, and this pain clouded my senses; I remained where I was, in silence.

Next to me, in a yellow puddle, was the bluish egg that had just been my trophy. A moment later, with a muffled thud, the whole nest came down to keep us company. The sight of this catastrophe made me feel stupid. It was the same feeling I'd had as I watched Leroy dine on the crow.

But I remembered the birds, and I hurried to be off. I got to my feet but could not any put weight on my left front paw. I took a few tentative steps, calculating how to move without giving myself too much pain.

The rain started up again, stronger and heavier than before, and by that time I had already gone some distance. A sharp crack of thunder stopped me in my tracks. Abruptly my mind took me back to the oak, the lost nest, the two birds in despair. When the rumbling stopped, I went back to limping through the woods.

"What's that?"

"Nothing."

"What did you do?"

"I fell. From a tree."

My siblings watched as our mother squeezed my paw. I shut my eyes and gritted my teeth, she was squeezing so hard.

"You idiot. You shit."

"I saw some eggs."

She let go of me and turned away toward the kitchen. The others were all sitting around the table.

"If you broke it, you're up the creek. You won't catch me calling the doctor."

They ate while I stood in a corner, curled against the wall. There was no plate set where I usually sat. The only one of them who looked at me more than once was Otis. Outside it continued to rain, in the dark, making an awful din.

Everything hurt, and I wept alone.

*

After two weeks I could tell I was getting better. I didn't feel any pain in my back anymore, but the pain in my paw remained like a curse. If I ran, it shot through me; if I put too much weight on the paw, it returned with a vengeance. Burdened by the shame of my uselessness, I found it almost impossible to accept that I was now lame. While I recovered, I spent my days in the bed with Otis and Cara, who did nothing but laze about there. I thought back on my recklessness, and the robins' eggs, and the desire for retaliation that I now had to put out of my mind. I often wept.

"Archy, does it hurt?" Otis asked me.

"No. I've got to die."

"If you've got to die, what will happen to me?"

He'd struggle up onto the bed and stare at me or try to catch Cara's eye. I ignored him, perhaps with some small degree of hatred, now that I saw I had more in common with him than with Leroy. My brother, the runt, the underfed weakling destined for a short life, had started talking to me.

As soon as I could, I left the den. I ran into Louise not far off.

"Archy, do you want to play?"

I couldn't keep up and soon lost sight of her. Louise scampered around the trees and stopped, then shot off again. When the pain got to be too much for me I lay down next to a thin little brook. A toad jumped in with a splash and hopped to the other side, looking at me lazily over his shoulder.

"Are you crying, Archy?"

It was Louise. She'd come back and was standing next to me, still catching her breath.

16

"Yes, I can't run anymore," I sobbed. The sound of the brook accompanied us for a long while, I went on weeping, and my sister stared across at the toad. Then, out of nowhere, she bit me on the ear and came at me. I rolled over on my back and bit her in turn, beginning to fight like usual. We tangled together furiously, then slowed down and quit hitting each other; the game had transformed into a gentle motion of bodies, in which I caressed her with my eyes closed, and a knot formed in my throat. Louise seemed to be experiencing the same sensation. She was breathing heavily, and her eyes were hazy.

She turned her back to me, letting me come closer to her. I climbed on top of her, gasping, as she pushed against me.

I felt the knot disappear; the world faded in an instant, and I was enfolded all around, in a shiver of heat. My sister cried out in pain, but she didn't move. Only then did I realize I'd slipped inside of her.

"Archy, Archy…" she asked, "am I beautiful, Archy?"

I said yes, but I think she hardly heard me.

Louise and I kept it up every day in that same place. She would wait for me by the brook and I would come hobbling to her. At night I did nothing but think of her, two bodies away to the left of me on the bed, sound asleep. I had forgotten my disgrace in the blink of an eye. Not even our mother's scornful looks could faze me.

"Maybe it would be better if we got out of here," I said to Louise as she lay next to me.

"Why?"

"I don't know. We could be on our own, forever."

She never listened to me.

"There's plenty of food at our mother's. And I like it here."

We didn't talk much. To restore our energy, we would lie on the stones in the stream with our eyes closed, or watch the sky grow dark. When we were ready we started homeward and slipped back into the den.

I used to have dreams about us running away together. That's why I'd ask her about it every now and then. In the dreams we would cross through the woods and head who knows where, delirious with happiness. When Louise talked to me about food I tumbled from the clouds, because in my fantasies I never pictured us eating, just running way out beyond everything. In fact, if we had run away, eating would have been more than necessary, and in my condition I couldn't have provided anything at all.

"It's the season of mating," she said, looking at herself in the water. "I love you, Archy."

3

A Hen and a Half

ONE MORNING my mother woke me up first thing. Leroy was already at the kitchen table, scarfing down some berries. She gave me some too.

"Mama—"

"Pipe down and eat."

Leroy gave me a superior look. He hadn't said a word to any of us since he'd proved he was an adult. We filed out of the den in silence. I was terrified they'd decided to kill me since a cripple was nothing but a burden; at any moment they'd attack me and serve me for dinner.

"Mama—"

"Come with us. And stop talking."

We went into the woods, past the Three Streams. I couldn't keep up with them, and my brother had to wait for me.

"Where are we going, Leroy?" I said.

But he just went on walking.

When it became clear to me that we'd gone too far, I stopped thinking that they were out to kill me. To curb my fear, I imagined they were taking me to the doctor, who would heal me and make me good as new. Ahead of us our mother waited at the edge of a meadow, among some trees that stood next to the tall grass, into which we all dove together. At the center of the meadow there was a small hill, on top of it a large boulder, and below this boulder a couple of little windows dug into the ground. Our mother knocked on one of these windows and someone saw her and came to open up the door. We filed into a very large, dark room filled with sacks of goods. The air smelled sweet. In one corner of this room, near the window our mother had knocked on, sat an old fox, illuminated by a small lamp. We stopped a few feet away from him.

"That him, Annette?" said the fox, pointing at me.

At this I shivered. I had never heard my mother's name before.

"Yes," she replied.

"He looks healthy."

"He's a cripple. He can't run. He's no use to me anymore."

The old fox laughed. "And to me he is?"

"He can work. You're old, and you won't find better."

I stared at my mother, straight into those dark eyes of hers. "Is he the doctor?"

She slapped me. I held my breath and hunched over, not saying anything more. Leroy looked on impassively.

"One hen, Annette, I won't give you more."

"A hen and a half, as we agreed."

The old fox stood up. "So be it. But the half after a month. And only if he works like you say he will."

Our mother didn't respond. The old fox went into another room and came back with a headless chicken. On one of the thighs was a mark I recognized, the mark of Solomon the lender. They were selling me to him for a hen and a half. They turned toward the door, but I clung to her.

20

"Mama!"

She pushed me away, and the hen fell to the ground.

"Don't cry, you shit!" she said, but I was crying already, gasping for breath. She picked up the hen and started for the door.

"Leroy!"

My brother didn't look at me.

"Mama! Mama! Forgive me, Mama!"

I thought of the nest and the tree and that loud crack of thunder.

"Enough, ass hair!" The old fox grabbed me by the scruff and lifted me off the ground. I writhed, I screamed like a lunatic, he hit me hard. We went through another room where he opened a small door that led into darkness.

"Get ahold of yourself, then we'll talk," he said. I screamed.

He prodded me in there, into the blackness, and shut the door behind him. The room was cramped. I pounded at the walls, trying to escape. I screamed until I had no more strength left to scream, and then I just wept, curled up into a ball. Never have I felt more lost, or weak, or invisible than I did in that moment.

I don't know how long I remained there, shut up in the dark, but there was time enough for me to fall asleep at least twice. All the familiar faces loomed before my eyes like dancing ghosts: first my mother, then Leroy and Cara, Otis and Louise.

Louise, in the season of mating. My breath grew faint. When the old fox opened the door, the light was blinding.

"Done whining, ass hair?"

I said nothing.

"It'll get better. Now get a move on."

He led me into a modest kitchen, yet another room. We sat at the table and he passed me a plate with a hollow bone and two grapes inside it.

"Eat, otherwise you've got to go."

I swallowed the two grapes. At which point I was done.

"What, you don't like the bone?" he said to me, pointing at it.

"It's empty, sir."

"I'm not *sir*. I'm your *master*. That's what you call me."

I nodded but still didn't touch the bone.

The old fox continued to stare at me.

"You're not stupid," he said, taking back the plate. "No, you're not stupid at all. You're Davis's son, right?"

I nodded again.

"He came to a bad end. On the other hand, there are only two things that stop a thief," he said. Then he got a worried expression and he looked me up and down. I shuddered seeing his features change like lightning.

"Say, you wouldn't be a thief, would you? In cahoots with your mother—do you think you can cheat me?"

I trembled. His gaze was hard and cutting, it passed right through me.

"No. Master."

The old fox stood up with a cry of satisfaction.

"All the better for you. And just call me sir."

He took me out of the den, up to the top of the little hill. We could see the whole meadow and the trees all around it.

22

"This is all mine. As far as you can see. Understand?"

"Yes, sir."

"Now I'll show you what you have to do."

The old fox pointed out a brook down in the valley and a little enclosure with some hens. Then he turned around and directed my gaze toward a cluster of plants, but by then I was already running. With uncertain, painful steps, urged on by fear, I'd almost reached the bottom of the hill and didn't stop. From behind me I heard a sharp whistle: Did the fox really think I'd halt at his command? Fat chance. I got as far as the tall grass, gritting my teeth to keep up the pace. The trees were close and it hardly mattered where I scrambled into them, I'd find the path once I'd covered my tracks. But just before I emerged from the tall grass something took my legs out from under me and knocked me down. I found myself face-to-face with an enormous dog. He held one paw against my chest so that I couldn't stand, gnashing his chipped teeth inches from my nose. I started to scream, but he bit me by the scruff and shook me like a rag. Though for a second I was sure I was being eaten alive, I quickly realized he was carrying me back up the hill.

"Ah! Like father like son! Both bastards!" said the old fox, waiting for the dog to bring me right to him. "Drop him, Joel!"

The dog let go of me and I fell to the ground.

"Do I look stupid to you, ass hair?" he said.

"No, sir."

"A liar. Just as I thought."

He hit me three times, hard, on the head. I screamed and started weeping.

"Let's kill him, Solomon. He's a coward, and a cripple to boot," said the dog.

The old fox stared him down. "Don't run your mouth. It always smells like shit, remember? Now go back to doing whatever you were doing before."

The dog trotted off as quiet as could be, without a word of protest. He jumped up onto the boulder and settled on the highest point.

The fox tied a tether around my neck.

"Now no more escape attempts, eh?"

He dragged me down the hillside toward the cluster of plants he'd pointed out earlier. He gave me a canvas sack and told me to fill it with wheat. When I'd done that, we went back over to the coop, where he made me give it to the chickens. Then we headed down to the brook with two empty buckets. One was for the hens, and the other for us.

Near the kitchen there was a big metal basin, which he forced me to fill, walking back and forth with the water. We went back again to the chickens to collect a few eggs and then proceeded to an apple tree at the far end of the meadow, where I filled another sack. At that point I was spent and the sun was sinking on the horizon. The old fox led me back into his den and removed the tether. My dinner was four grapes and an egg.

"Tired?" he said.

"Yes, sir."

"All right. To bed with you then."

I was shut up again in the lightless little cell. I understood that this was going to be my room for who knew how long. In spite of my exhaustion, I couldn't sleep; I tossed and turned in the dark, not closing my eyes, contemplating the blackness all around me. I was thinking about Louise. She was the only one I missed, and she seemed so far away.

*

In the days that followed the old fox continued to keep me on a tether. He had fashioned a much longer one and carried a chair with him so that he could be comfortable while he watched me work. He criticized me constantly.

The tasks I performed remained more or less the same, but at times they changed. He made me cut the grasses in the valley and chop wood for the stove and plant seeds near the wheat. He would not explain things more than once and got angry if I made a mistake or showed that I was tired. He pulled hard on the tether so that it burned my neck. I wept and grew even angrier.

"Stop crying, ass hair!"

He said he couldn't stand me, I made him feel soft.

"Try and act like you're not a weakling, please."

We spoke very little. There were days when I wouldn't say a word, it seemed I'd yawned my tongue away. During the hours I spent working, all I did was remember. Every now and then I thought back to the days I'd spent in the big bed with the others, and once, I recalled the time our mother had taken Joshua away because he'd started to stink. Even though he was dead, he'd been my brother for a few days, we had kept each other warm.

"Look what you're doing. You've dropped half a bucket's worth. Dump it out and go back."

It wasn't easy living in memories. Not when you were already busy doing something else, as I was. The only advantage to torment-ing myself like that was coming to understand my feelings more fully. I discovered that Louise, except on the banks of that brook, didn't exist for me. I never wondered how she was at that moment, or if she missed me, or if she was in pain. It was clear to me that the very powerful bond between her and me was that moment of pleasure we'd experienced, and beyond that there was nothing. I don't know why, but I felt sad. A prisoner of sunlight and darkness, indifferent to the days.

"Hurry up with that water!"

The old fox knew how to listen. One morning at the table he asked me how it was in my room.

"It's dark, sir," I said. He did not respond. That evening I found a lamp by my bed, already lit. There were no windows in that cell, which was why it was so pitch-black.

If I did my work well no one mistreated me, and I was given something in return. One day I made almost no mistakes and at dinner I received a chicken thigh with the meat around the bone. Others followed.

"Do you know that God almost made Abraham kill Isaac?"

The old fox would frequently say things like this. I didn't know God or Isaac, or for that matter Abraham, and did not understand. I imagined these were stories from his past.

"Do you know that he created the world in seven days?"

I would have liked him to explain further, but I was afraid he wouldn't appreciate my curiosity. When he talked to me like that I held my tongue, and he retreated into his thoughts.

His clients showed up at odd hours. All the animals of the forest came through there. Badgers and rabbits, foxes and rodents, even wild cats. If they crossed paths, it was Joel's duty to keep the peace. In the meadow the rules were different. No one ate anyone.

"A dead client isn't good for business," the old fox used to say.

They would come into the den with nothing or with something. They would state what they needed or the payment they were going to discharge. The old fox would pick up a wooden board and mark some lines with some color, covering the board with incomprehensible signs. Not a single day's delay escaped him, nor the slightest debt, even if it was no more than one seed. Everyone made his payments on time. If he didn't, Joel was out looking for them. Before the deal was struck, the client turned over a tuft of his fur. This was important, for the scent. If he still hadn't paid when his time was up, the dog would take that tuft and disappear into the woods; he would come back with what was owed or with the owner. No one tried anything funny with Solomon the lender.

To break up the silence, I befriended the hens. I talked; they didn't know how. They'd come up to me to take the feed from the sack, and I'd start jabbering at them.

"Are you turning into a chicken, ass hair? You're ridiculous."

The old fox found it very funny when he caught me chatting with the chickens, but only for a little while. The longer I kept it up, the more irritated he became. For three days he said nothing, acted like nothing was happening. Then on the evening of the fourth day he dragged me to the coop.

"It's been a month," he said. "Today is the second week of summer, and your mother will be wanting her half a hen." He looked in and pointed to a black one. "That one there. Snap her neck and bring her here."

I flinched, because he'd chosen my favorite. I'd named her Sara and let her eat from my paw. Sara was a beauty.

"If you weep, you'll get a beating."

27

It took me a while even to make a move in her direction. Sara hustled toward me, even though I had nothing for her. I had never killed, and fear made me tremble.

"Sara, my beauty," I said, stroking her. The hen let herself be touched. She was used to it.

"Why don't we get this show on the road?" the old fox urged. He yanked on the tether, burning my neck. I held Sara in my arms, and she did not rebel. I could hardly choke back my tears. It wasn't clear to me what I was supposed to do. I bit her head and pulled hard, my teeth pierced her bones, I felt them crack in my mouth. Sara spluttered desperately, flapping her wings, as I went on mauling her.

"Around her neck, stupid! It'll take you till tomorrow to kill her that way!"

In that moment my fear dissolved. It was like I was back on the branches of the dead tree with the robins' nest; free from all thought, I was acting on an indomitable desire, urged on by the blood. I ripped Sara's head clean off, and her body began running around the coop. Having killed one chicken, I could have killed them all, and it took an effort not to start chasing them right there and then. Sara's body fell to the ground and I spit out her head. Abruptly my euphoria vanished and I discovered I was wheezing, scared and happy at the same time. I retrieved her body and fetched it back to the old fox. Tears, much as I tried to restrain them, streamed down my snout.

"Done with the kit stuff?" he said.

"Yes, sir." I sobbed.

He raised his paw, and I moved to ward off a blow, but he was only removing the tether from around my neck.

"Let's go," he said.

We headed back toward the hill, Sara's body swaying with each step the old fox took.

I wasn't afraid anymore, but I went on weeping from joy.

4

Before, After, Wasps

THE DAY AFTER THAT I worked by myself, with no one keeping an eye on me. I did my chores as usual without any attempt at escape, resisting the urge. The old fox conversed with a couple of clients, then went outside with his chair to soak up the sun. He looked satisfied.

"Well done, Chicken!" he barked at me.

I was content. *Chicken* was better than *ass hair*. I felt I was becoming strong all of a sudden, a real animal. My paw was hurting me, but I ignored it, I didn't start crying; I concentrated all my thoughts on what I was doing.

"You know what God did to the Egyptians?"

I was walking past him with the water bucket.

"He cast ten plagues upon them! Water changed into blood, frogs, mosquitoes . . . and the others I don't remember."

We dined on one half of Sara at the table, where Joel also sat.

"I'm tired of cooking," said the old fox. "I'll have to teach Chicken once he sharpens up."

We sat there in silence.

"Tell me about the badgers." He was looking at the dog now.

"Fosco is ill, he has blood in his mouth."

"I see. And?"

"They don't think he's going to make it. The eldest son asked for five days."

The old fox spat out a bone. "What's his name?"

"Salvo."

"And this Salvo, does he know the way?"

The badger's son knew where to make the payment. The old fox made up his mind that he was reliable, and five days to pull it together seemed feasible. Obviously, though, this extra time would make a slight difference to the total—a detail that Joel said he'd already communicated. The old fox launched into a speech about the respect other animals had for him. He said that fear made them reliable, like dawn in the morning, but not more intelligent.

"And a good thing too," he concluded.

When the plates were empty he motioned for me to collect them.

"Tomorrow bring the half hen down to the beech martens by Zò's," he said to the dog.

Joel gestured with his head. "And how am I supposed to find them? I've never been there."

The old fox shook himself slightly. His eyes cast around for an answer. "Ah, that's right. Annette isn't in debt." He thought another moment.

"Take him with you."

I pointed to myself and responded with a start, pricking up my ears.

"You know how to get to your mother's place, Chicken?"

"More or less, sir."

Something gnawed at my stomach. My heart pounded in my

temples. An image of the den and the big bed drifted through my mind. I felt happy, then curious, then plummeted into an indecipherable whirl. Louise stood before my eyes, accompanied by the sound of water. I tried to work out if I was simply happy to be getting away from the hill.

"If he makes a break for it, you kill him and that's that. And bring the rest of the hen back too." The old fox wrapped up what he had to say to Joel. "You'll make sure, however, that he doesn't make a break for it. You're not running off now, are you, Chicken?"

"No, sir. Anyway, I'm a cripple."

He laughed. "Exactly."

We set out the next day toward evening, once my chores were done. The old fox marked the half hen with some color and gave it to the dog. At the far end of the meadow my companion stopped to speak to me.

"We'll head toward the Fields of Zò. As soon as you remember where you are, you lead the way."

I agreed. Then I cast glances behind me as the hill hid behind the trees.

Joel trotted at a modest enough pace that I was able to keep up with him without having to strain myself. Joel may have been the one who had to strain to go slow. He kept leaving me in the dust, then coming back and trotting over the path with me again with amiable, wordless patience. He was no longer the ruthless jailer at the beck and call of our common master, and I soon felt at ease. After a while, summoning my courage, I endeavored to make the journey even more pleasant.

"Where are you from, Joel?" it occurred to me to say. The night was now caressing our eyes.

The dog looked at me for an instant and then proceeded on his way. I'd started to regret having said a word when he roused himself as if from a dream.

"From a wasps' nest."

The answer baffled me as much as the fact that I'd received it.

"What?" I said.

"Solomon found a wasps' nest near his den, pulled it down, and broke it open. That's how I came into this world, and ever since he's kept me around."

I had never heard such a story. I remember I kept very quiet for a while, trying to imagine how wasps could engender a dog.

"I just come from my mother," I said at last.

Joel nodded but said nothing more.

When we topped a small hill, I recognized the Three Streams. From that point on I led the way, shivering every time I saw a detail from my memories. I passed right by the bush where I'd lain in wait, and it stirred up all the sensations I'd felt back then, crushed between the branches. The trees, although altered by the season and distorted by the darkness, seemed fresh from my thoughts. As did the smells and some familiar sounds.

I realized I was slowing my pace as I contemplated that strange journey backward, that confrontation between before and after, that distance I had never considered before.

"What is it? What's going on?" said the dog.

I came back to my senses. Dazed but alert. "Nothing. It's this way."

We went quickly on.

33

*

My mother's den soon loomed in the distance. The two trees nearby were covered with rattling leaves, and the grass had grown up at the entrance. From the small window, together with the light from inside, someone was peering out. The sight of Cara's mutilated face gave me a little shiver of excitement. Perhaps she recognized me too, although she remained completely still.

We stopped.

"I can't go in there. I'm too big," said Joel. He took the half hen and gave it to me. "You'd better hurry."

I nodded and dived in.

It was smaller than I remembered. Cramped, poor. The roof was so low it forced me to hunch, and it was colder inside than outdoors. These considerations, however, occupied me only for the briefest of moments. The whole household was sitting at the table, finishing their meal. My mother, in her usual place; Louise, as beautiful as she was in my dreams; and a figure I had never seen. He sat where I used to sit. They all stopped and looked in my direction.

He was an adult marten with dark fur and a massive head. He kept his wide paw flat on the table, his jaw still working on the last mouthful. His eyes were pinned, determined, on me. Only then did I realize that the smell of the den was different.

"What the hell is this?" my mother slurred.

I pulled myself together and looked at her. I knew that she recognized me, her eyes were full of scorn, it was the only expression we'd ever shared.

"My master sends you half a hen," I muttered, and held up the meat as if proof were needed.

"About time," she said, "put it in there," and she pointed to the kitchen.

But I didn't budge.

"Who's this?"

I would never have let myself ask the question if I hadn't been so out of sorts. My mother's eyes went wide.

"Mind your own damn business, you shit! Stick that hen in the kitchen and get out of here!"

It was as if I hadn't spoken. And all the while I went on observing that squalid little room. Cara hadn't even turned her head.

"Where's Leroy? And Otis?"

My mother stood up and took a swipe at me. Half of Sara fell to the floor, and I fell with her.

"Are you deaf? I told you to get out of here!"

"Mama," I murmured, but another blow rained down.

In pain and confusion, I looked up at Louise, still sitting at the table, staring at me.

"Hi, Archy," she said softly.

A long moment went by. I got to my feet again, and without taking my eyes off my sister tried to work out what her expression was trying to say. Her darting glances, her half-folded ears, her wavering mouth; there were too many things that were neither one thing nor the other—a weave of happiness and fear, turmoil and silence. Looking at her face, I found it impossible to imagine having talked with her, having been close to her, having joined together. I felt I didn't know who she was, yet whatever she was trying to convey to me was struggling to the surface there, in my memories.

My mother bit me by the scruff and pushed me to the entrance. To keep her from doing it twice I scurried off, rushing out of there, and she did not pursue me. She had punctured my flesh, but the confusion I was feeling prevailed over the pain. Joel was there waiting for me.

"Let's go," he said.

"Please, just a moment."

The dog studied me. I thought he would ignore what I said, but instead he sat down and gestured that it was all right.

I turned back toward my mother's den. Cara was still staring out the window. In a few steps, I was face-to-face with her, hunched down so that the others wouldn't notice me. I could see the stranger finishing his dinner.

"Cara, it's me, can you see me?" I whispered.

"I see you," she replied in a still small voice.

"What's going on?"

"Wait."

She turned and left the window. After a while she emerged from the den, moving slowly, like a creature deprived of sight. We went over by Joel.

"They think I'm blind. If they didn't, chances are they would have kicked me out already."

Cara still had the same sullen face and cold, detached voice she'd acquired the day that she lost her eye.

"His name is Mathias. But to us he's Papa. Ever since he came around, a lot of things have changed."

She began to tell the tale, and I listened closely. Joel did too, covertly pricking his ears, perhaps convinced I hadn't noticed. My sister's bitter words captivated us both.

Mathias had shown up in our mother's den a few days after my departure. No one knew where he came from or what had befallen him before he appeared. He was younger than our mother, you could tell by his coat and his aggressiveness, and by the ease with which he fell asleep. They'd come home together, but they must have gotten to know each other sometime earlier, perhaps in the woods, while she was on the hunt. He had fallen in love with her, Mama may have expected nothing less, and she hadn't objected. The season of mating permeates the air like pollen. Our mother laughed with him, and doted on him, and relaxed her pinched snout; it was as if she'd harbored this transformation within her all her life. Suddenly she was silly, her head full of dreams.

She became crueler with her children. She called them "bastards," told them to pipe down and make themselves scarce. If they'd disappeared into thin air, she would have been glad, but still she went on bringing them food. The sight of my brothers made her eyes go dead; she fell into herself—into a sad familiar emptiness hidden away inside her.

The smell of the males made Mathias nervous. He got into a fight with Leroy on the bed and chased him out, telling him not to come back. The next day he'd picked up Otis and carried him out of the den. Otis had been ill for a few days, short of breath. He never got out of bed, found it hard to eat, and was becoming even smaller and more misshapen.

He would be gone in no time, and yet out into the woods they went. Mathias told him to choose a path and walk, but Otis didn't move. He remained outside through the night, weeping, and through the next day, never coming back inside. When he was stiff, our mother took him away.

It was around this time the females had to start calling him Papa. He liked Louise, caressed her secretly when Mama wasn't looking, but was very careful. Cara decided to pretend she'd gone blind so as not to put him on edge. If he realized she knew what was going on he would send her away, or perhaps kill her. He had let her stay in the den so that he wouldn't have to kick both of them out. Cara knew her survival depended on being as invisible as possible, just as Louise knew she mustn't breathe a word. Cara stuck to the window: as long as something ended up on her plate, it was all fine by her.

Mathias did not hunt, he let our mother go alone. Once she was gone he took Louise and they disappeared into the woods, silent and anxious, like you are when you steal something. They came home one at a time, first her and then him, or the other way around; Mama wasn't usually back yet, but if she was he would tell her that he'd gone to eat berries, and he was always believed.

Cara took a long pause.

"Beyond that I don't have anything to tell you," she said. "As you've seen, no one here can relate to your memories, or even to their own."

She turned around, walking with the hesitant step of the blind. Joel started off, and I joined him as soon as I saw her at the window. The night was dark and we made our way quickly, or at least I tried to keep up a good pace. Something disappeared with every step I took. All the exhilaration of the journey, the thrill of returning, of recognizing the woods, faded into nothing. The big bed, the den, Louise at the brook, the robins' nest—they were all being swept away by a strong current. Before and After hadn't come together; one had drowned out the other, negating the difference. My sisters and mother wore the face of Mathias, and Leroy and Otis had disappeared, along with everything else, like dreams that slip away on waking.

Joel noticed me chewing it over.

"If you were born of wasps, you wouldn't give it so much thought," he said.

He wasn't wrong. Yet it seemed to me he looked sad.

5

God

THE FOLLOWING DAYS PASSED SLOWLY. For long moments at
a stretch, in the middle of my chores, I found myself spellbound,
I stared into space, and I made more mistakes than usual. I was still
disoriented from the journey and the loss of my memories. Out of
nowhere, the odor that I'd smelled inside the den would come and
sting my nostrils. If I had a thought about Louise, Mathias was there
too. Cara's face at the window, the same as it was when I first ventured out into the forest, drifted farther and farther away, as it had
the last time I'd seen her.

"You slacking off, Chicken? Nostalgic for your family?" the old
fox shouted at me.

I shook my head no. I wasn't nostalgic for anything.

Five days after my journey, as Joel had reported, the badger's son
arrived in the meadow with the payment due. He climbed the hill
and came into the den. At that moment I'd just finished filling the
big basin in the kitchen with water. He set down two sacks of vegetables and one of seeds at the old fox's feet.

"How's your father faring?"

"Not well at all."

Solomon grunted. "And the interest?"

The young badger rooted around in one of the sacks and produced a small box. It was made of wood, with colored carvings. Instantly the old fox's eyes lit up, and he snatched it lightning quick out of the young badger's paws. He hunched over it as though he wanted to eat it, edging away. He was studying it intently.

"Where did you get this?" he spluttered.

"I don't know. It's my father's."

"Fine, fine. We're good, you can go, debt settled." He spoke without looking up. The young badger prepared to leave. "You want a hen? Some wheat?" the old fox muttered distractedly.

The young badger stopped at the threshold. "No, thank you."

The old fox was still contemplating the object. "We'll talk about it later, the summer is short."

When we were alone again, I nosed closer to him.

"What is it?"

He jumped in fright, perhaps not realizing I was in the den. He clutched the box to him as he took his eyes off it.

"What are you doing in here? Get to work!" he shouted.

At that point I was the one who frightened myself.

"I've already put the water in the basin, sir," I squeaked.

"Your nose is longer than your tail, ass hair!"

He breezed past me into his room, shutting himself inside. I picked up the bags of seeds and vegetables, put them away, and went back to my chores.

During the days that followed the old fox made himself scarce. He left his room only if there was a client or when it was time to eat. Even then he brought the box to the table and went on staring at it, immersed, between one bite and the next, touching it every now and then. He seemed to be petitioning it for something, an answer to a desire that was troubling him. I hardly paid any attention to my plate either. I would pretend to be looking at nothing in particular, but my eyes were always pinned on the other side of the table.

Behind the old fox's paw, I could see the colored carvings on the sides of the box. On one I recognized a picture of animals fighting; on two others they were in furious pursuit. On the fourth side, when the old fox turned it in my direction, I saw two creatures that I had never seen before, very tall ones, standing close together. They were white and stared off into the distance. I rarely saw that picture because he always kept it facing him.

"What's the matter, you're not hungry?"

"I am hungry, sir. I'm eating."

I went back to my plate. Then I waited for him to lose himself in thought again, so that I could strain to see what I could see.

Often he left half his food untouched. He got up and disappeared into his room, shutting the door behind him. He left me by myself to tidy up, and before long I was quite practiced at it.

I'd never gone into his room or seen where he slept. The first few days I'd gotten a bit of a glimpse through the half-open door, but I hadn't dared to poke around. I had no doubt the old fox went on turning the box over and over between his paws even as he lay in bed, bound by his own private spell. At night, when he left me by myself, the big den was all mine. I wandered around the rooms and sat in his chair under the little window by the entrance, eating grapes. I imagined Mathias, and Louise's face. I imagined I was in a kingdom of my own.

"Make us some food, Chicken."

The old fox never took his eyes off the box. I flinched, but I wasn't too frightened: I'd watched him cook so many times that I was sure I could manage.

"What should I make, sir?" I asked just the same.

"One egg and one tomato apiece. Get to it now, and pipe down." He slammed his paw on the table. "I've got to understand this. I cannot not understand it."

He was talking to himself, but I decided to pounce on those words just the same.

"What?" I murmured.

The old fox turned on me, gnashing his teeth, the fur on his head bristling.

"Why don't you pipe down when I ask you to? I already told you to keep your nose out of it!"

He threw his plate at me, missing me by an inch. I skittered into a corner of the room.

"Make some food and pipe down, ass hair!" He got to his feet. "When I order you to do something, you do what I say, we're not pals, got it?"

Perhaps he'd risen awkwardly to his feet, but for whatever reason the table gave a jump and the box fell to the ground. The noise drilled into my ears, piercing my every vein like a breath of ice. The old fox stopped dead, stunned, his eyes motionless and wide. My heart thrashed in my chest, my breath made my head spin; I felt the tears coming, and terror too. I flattened myself into the corner.

Suddenly a sound I'd never heard rang out in the room. Quick clangs resonating in the air one after the other, but each of them different. They whirled together, up and down, creating a delicate noise that caressed the ears. The box had opened, and a figure similar to the ones carved on the side began to move in circles, accompanying the noise. We stood there staring at it for a good long while, rapt and frozen to the spot.

"Ah!" the old fox exclaimed. "Ah!"

He bent down to pick it up and raised it to eye level. Slowly the lid closed itself, and the hidden figure danced back inside. When it was completely closed, the noise ceased. Solomon waited a moment, then reopened the cover, starting it up all over again.

"Ah!" he said.

I wrenched myself out of the corner. The noise soothed me, as did the old fox's blissful expression.

"What is it?" I said to him, spellbound.

He smiled at me. "This is the secret! This is the function! This is man!" he shouted.

He went into his room, taking the noise in there with him. I tidied up the kitchen and ate by myself.

Summer scorched the meadow grass. It turned yellow and rattled in the wind. Work was harder in the heat, I panted and closed my eyes, and went down more often to the brook to drink. When it got too hot I sat in the shade of the big boulder, weaving baskets or making sacks. The old fox stayed inside the den attending to his accounts, completely recovered now from his love for the box, which had disappeared into his room. For days after it had opened up, he'd gone on listening to it over and over, so many times that I learned the noise by heart and memorized the movements of that spinning

44

figure. One day, while I was loitering in the shade, Joel came up from the meadow with a dead rabbit in his mouth. He fetched up beside me to catch his breath and dropped the rabbit on the ground.

"Who's that?" I asked him.

"One of Tito's sons."

"Who's Tito?"

"Someone who didn't pay."

The body of the little rabbit was twisted and bloody. He was missing some fur around his neck, and his face was still frozen in a silent scream. Joel stared intently at the treetops at the far end of the meadow while his breath slowly returned to normal. Probably Tito had made a run for it, and so Joel had to settle for prey closer to hand; or perhaps Joel had killed Tito's son on purpose to try to force him to pay off his debt. I knew very little about what Joel got up to when he wasn't in the meadow. There was no doubt, however, that he did anything that the old fox told him to do.

The question came to me without thinking. "Do you know who God is?"

Joel didn't take his eyes off the trees. "The father of men."

I was amazed. Joel knew God, and God was the father of men. Who knows how many children he had.

"How did you get to know him?" I pressed.

"How did you?" he answered.

"I don't know him. Solomon talks about him."

"Exactly."

We sat there in silence. I thought the conversation was over, but the dog turned to face me.

"Solomon has a thing in his room. He keeps it hidden, but I know it was thanks to that thing that he got to know God."

45

Before I could say anything further, Joel had already picked up the rabbit in his mouth. He trotted off toward the entrance to the den, where he was going to show the old fox what had come of his outing. He left me more curious than ever. I went back to making baskets.

The first autumn leaf fell right under my nose while I was gathering fallen apples. The foliage faded slowly, turned red and yellow, and the wind changed direction. I was still growing, I had filled out and become strong, I was working during the day and making food in the evening.

At night I thought about the old fox's secrets, torn between fear and desire, wondering when and how I might sneak into his room and poke around. I tried to remember the faint noise of the box, which I'd already forgotten, then I fell asleep and dreamed vivid dreams.

The old fox had me start collecting firewood for winter. He said it was a work of cunning, because you had to take time by surprise. I ventured out beyond the meadow and gathered fallen twigs, harvested dead branches, and was always on the lookout for bigger and bigger ones.

"This will burn up in a second. Winter lasts a hundred days. You want to keep warm for a second, Chicken?"

He threw the ones he didn't like back at me, but I dodged them fairly well.

"Do you know what happened to the man who collected wood on the Sabbath?"

I wished I did.

One windy day I found him sitting by the window, eating grapes. I went back and forth with the water bucket, right past him. The sixth time I came back he was asleep, and it seemed to me he might go on sleeping that way forever, his eyes closed and his breath slow, harmless to everyone around him, with not a word to say. I set down the bucket and stole off toward his room without a second thought.

Light came in through an underground window, impossible to detect from outside. There was a big bed and an unlit lamp and piles of strange stuff along the walls. The air smelled cool and ancient, arousing my curiosity, which grew stronger as I moved around the room. I observed absurd metal tools, objects with ineffable mechanisms, and hand-drawn depictions of those same mysterious white creatures. On a small table I recognized the box in a jumble of little things, which seemed somehow more important than the others. The temptation to open it wasn't easy to ignore.

I had no idea what object in particular I was seeking, nor could I imagine a tool that would let me get to know God. I had to find something that had been hidden away, that was all I knew.

"Lousy bastard coward and deceiver!"

I spun around. The old fox, chewing on a grape, stared at me from the doorway. Rage made him puff out his belly.

"Are you stealing from me? Eh? What are you up to?"

In three steps he was on top of me. I tried to curl up into a ball as best I could, protecting my head with my paw.

"I'm looking for God!" I screamed.

He hit me hard, and then again, and again. "May God strike you dead! Thief! Ass hair!" he spit.

I screamed in pain and started weeping.

"You weak whining son of no one! You're looking for God? Here's

47

God for you!" The old fox hit me again, then suddenly stopped. After a little while, I lifted my head and saw him wide-eyed, bending backward, with both paws clasped around his throat. His mouth was open, but all he produced were muted gurglings, which came in waves. Though the pain was still searing, I stood. His eyes leapt at me, desperate, and with one paw he grabbed at my fur.

"Sir…" I whispered.

He squeezed tight, then slid to the ground, still struggling with himself. At that point I leaned over him and began to shake him, as if to drive away some invisible opponent. The old fox flailed, contorted, while I went on pulling at him. Suddenly he coughed and gasped for air. He spat out two small grape seeds, then kept on coughing until he frothed at the mouth and the snot bubbled from his nose. His eyes slowly returned to his sockets, his paws caressing his throat. When he was breathing regularly again, we lay there in silence for a long time. He was staring into a corner of the room, trembling.

"Sir…"

"Get out of here," he wheezed. He didn't have to tell me twice.

For six days the old fox withdrew into silence. He did not punish me in any way, nor did he give the impression of being angry. He went outside with his chair and stared into the distance, sitting there all day, until the sun went down. He sent his clients away and told them to come back another time. If he did not shuffle in when darkness fell, I would go out with a plate that he almost always left untouched. His eyes were lost in desperate agitation. His face hardened into a frown, and his paws hung limp.

48

I could not stop wondering what had happened. In my imagination, I pieced it all together and pinned the blame on God. Perhaps the old fox thought he was being punished, like the Egyptians or the man who collected firewood on the Sabbath. He had beaten me and God had punished him. I had gone looking for God and he had stood in my way. These thoughts led me back to the door of his room, but by then he had blocked it.

On the sixth day, when I brought him his plate, I saw that he was crying.

Tears drenched his muzzle, and he sighed unashamedly, in a broken voice.

He turned to face me as I passed him the plate.

"I don't want it," he said.

He drew a deep breath and calmed himself, put a paw over his eyes. The night illuminated his gritted teeth.

The following morning I found him in the kitchen, curled up into a ball.

He must not have slept a wink, and his plate was still where I'd left it. Quietly I fixed something to eat.

"What is your name?"

I turned to him. He looked at me gravely.

"I'm Chicken," I replied, holding still, as though he needed a chance to recognize me.

"That's what I call you. What name did your mother give you?"

"Archy, sir."

The old fox merely nodded.

"You want to get to know God, Archy?" he asked.

A chill ran through me and I paused.

"Yes, sir. If you allow it."

He laughed. For a moment the gloom left his face.

"You're not stupid. It's a good thing."

I sat down. The old fox slid an object I'd never seen before out from under his rump. It was rectangular, black, with some gold carvings on the surface. With a dull thud, he placed it on the table, brushing aside his plate. I craned my neck to get a better look, but he put his paw on top of it.

"You know what death is, Archy?"

I stared at him. With his eyes, he begged me to answer.

"It's when others go away. They go to sleep forever."

The old fox smiled bitterly.

"Death is the primal will of God," he said in a broken voice. "And others don't have anything to do with it, because it happens to all of us."

He clenched his paw into a fist and two tears trickled down his snout.

"I will die, I have known it for a long time. God has willed it, just as he has willed that you will die too."

The blood froze in my veins. For a moment I was seized by an abject fear, rooted deep in my soul, which ordered me to leave that room and run. I decided not to listen to it and stayed put, though I could feel my body going rigid. The old fox wiped away his tears.

"That's how it is," he said. "The last day comes for us all. If somebody had told me this when I was young, I would never have believed it."

And so, to keep from being engulfed by this absurd awareness, I began to think. I cast back over my life up to that point and counted how many times it had crossed my mind that I might die. Not once. Death had always touched those around me, never me; in my existence I ruled it out in advance, forgotten behind the progression of the days, which I believed would continue on forever without end. Now I was subdued by an invisible force. The weight of the air and the earth beneath my paws, the weight of the sky and the forest and all the rivers came to crush me beneath it. I broke in two.

I gritted my teeth, took a quick breath, and with my heart battering my ribs I started weeping too.

"I don't believe it," I murmured. "I don't want to."

The old fox took one side of the object in front of him and opened it. Inside, there were a large number of thin strips bound together, covered with symbols I'd never seen before carved in horizontal lines.

"It says so here, it is the word of God. Everyone has an end."

"Who is God?"

"He is the father of the world." The old fox wiped away his tears again. "The only one who does not die."

6

Apprenticeship

THE OLD FOX decided to teach me all that he knew. The object on the table, the word of God, he told me to call a book, and the signs in it he told me to call writing. In order to understand what the signs said it was necessary to learn to read. Once I learned to read, I would also learn to write. The old fox knew how to do both of these things, and considering I'd become his apprentice, he said there was no need any longer to call him sir, but simply Solomon.

It took me a few days to get started. The tremendous revelation of death robbed me of sleep, sapped my strength, and left me drowning in silent desperation. Everything I saw gave me pain, everything I heard faded away from me like an odious echo; my whole connection with life had disappeared behind my awareness of its end. Otis came to me in my dreams, and I thought about him when I was awake. I remembered his words to our mother, when he was sitting at the table with us: "I'm going to die because I'm not growing."

Sad as he was, drenched in tears, he hadn't seemed quite sure of what he was saying, not as sure as Solomon had been. It was still a kit's caprice, an innocent lament full of hope: even Otis didn't believe his life would end. Now that I knew my brother's fate, mine and everyone else's was clear. I would never have supposed that this was a world in which I could die. But now I had to die, and the world spoke to me and said that it was not mine.

During those few days the old fox didn't force me to do my usual chores. He cooked for us both and made no attempt to cheer me up. He himself was feeling better, even in a good mood. When he realized my gloom was slow to lift, he began talking to me before he went off to bed.

"You kill death, you know, if you don't think about it."

I stared at him. "Why's that?"

"Why's that? Because it isn't here and now. If I, decrepit as I am, don't give it any thought, why should you?"

I lay down to sleep in my cell. Grasping those words, a part of me took a leap forward and I puffed up my chest. It wasn't long before I was feeling better.

Solomon gave me a ragged book fashioned from a cloth similar to the sacks I sewed. It was his creation, he told me with pride. Inside there was a comprehensive list of the symbols I needed to learn—the letters that together formed words—drawn in the same color he used to mark his goods. In the evening, when the housework was done, we would sit in the kitchen and study them. When we came to certain sounds the old fox seemed a bit uncertain, and if I pointed this out to him he lost his temper and said that they were open to interpretation. But I grasped things quickly, and this pleased him. Even though I'd worked all day, I put whatever energy I had left into my studies, I asked questions, I made myself repeat it all again and again. When I learned to distinguish the letters, we moved on to words and their meanings.

"In the beginning God created the heavens and the earth."

This was the first sentence that he had me read. Halting and ragged as my reading was, my master was moved.

"And that's how it's done," he said.

He taught me with great care, fighting off his weariness. He did not rush me or skip passages. I could see that he harbored a secret enthusiasm within him, a gentle fury for which I could not account. When there were meanings I didn't grasp, he paused to explain them, often with reference to other rules; when he saw me getting tired, we took a break; when I became curious about something, he encouraged me. I had developed a certain confidence in him, and he didn't give me the cold shoulder. We began to talk differently, like two equals, moved by kindred intentions. One evening I conquered my greatest fear and asked him how he came to know God, and how he was able to teach me all that he was teaching me. The old fox stared at me, not saying a word, and a terrible shiver ran through me.

"When I was young I was a bandit and did not have a den," he began.

I breathed a sigh of relief and pricked up my ears.

Solomon made his living as a thief, scrambling from place to place, always on the run. Other animals hired him to steal for them, or to kill an old enemy, paying him with whatever he needed. There was no bandit shrewder than he, or half as wretched, and none with so much spirit.

One day, as he was roving about, he saw a man hanging from a tree. The man didn't move or speak, so Solomon, undaunted, crept closer to him. He tasted a piece of him, taking bites as he swayed, another, and then another. He was clinging to the man, trying to climb higher, when something fell and hit him on the head. Frightened and in pain, he scampered off a ways, but soon he returned, as did the silence. The fallen object commanded his attention and made its value known from the first, speaking to him in secret. It beckoned to him, it seemed, in a faraway and yet familiar voice. And so he took the object with him.

At first he couldn't make heads or tails of it. He couldn't fathom letters, let alone words. The thing remained a mystery, a nightly torment that robbed him of sleep. If it had fallen on his head, from the heavens, there must be a reason. Never in his life had he sought any sense deeper than his instinct alone.

That was when he began to spy on men. He watched what they did and how they talked, trying to understand. He met a dog who took a liking to him. Her owner's children were learning to read and write, so she too could understand a bit. He brought her the thing he had caught in the woods and she instructed him, pledging to keep a close ear on the children.

Once he could read, the word of God hit him over the head even more forcefully. The truth about life and the world destroyed everything that up till then he had been, eradicating his very self. For several days, like me, he'd been on the verge of giving in to death. Then he got back on his feet. If God had chosen to reveal these things to him, there could only be one explanation.

"I am his son. I am a man," he said.

I remained frozen to the spot. I peered into his wide-open eyes.

"A man?" I stammered.

"Yes," he whispered. "He's done it to others before, you know. He transformed me." He looked down at his paws as if he were seeing them for the first time. "I am a man, otherwise he wouldn't have singled me out. I am his son."

He sat there in silence, thinking who knows what.

"Why did he do this to you?" I asked.

"I don't know, but it doesn't matter," he said, smiling. "Men are always saved."

We went back to our reading. His words whirled in my head. And with them the certainty that I was only an animal.

God created the earth, the heavens, and a large lake called the sea. He conceived Adam and Eve, who in turn conceived mankind. The Hebrews were his people, and he made them fight with other people who did not know him or who repudiated him. Many passages in the book recounted remote and not very interesting stories, which confused me. God was good, and he was angry. He punished those who obeyed him, and he remained silent to those who sought him. Men had to worship him and respect his laws, and anyone who behaved well could go to Heaven.

This was the place, remote from the world, where God resided, and where spirits went to find him after death. Solomon put a great deal of stock in this place, because he had been a man.

Animals did not end up anywhere, and this filled me with anguish.

"What about animals who know God?"

"You'd have to ask him."

Winter had had the forest in its grip for several days. Now and then a bit of snow fell, settling on the snow that was already on the ground. Solomon gave me another room, a bigger one, with a window. He did not ask for thanks and said they used to keep the chickens in there when it got too cold. We stood by the fire, in the kitchen, taking the wood from the pile I had made.

"I don't covet the women of others. And what is a woman?"

"It is a female man."

Solomon went on telling me stories about his life, if I knew when to ask. He had turned to lending not long after he'd discovered God, thanks to his teachings.

"From them I learned that life wasn't just stealing. Or killing," he said.

It seemed to me that he was still stealing and killing, but using a more complex system, which, he said, he had also learned from God's book.

When the weather turned bitterly cold he'd send me up to Joel with a basket of wood. The dog's den was in a hole in the boulder, above our heads. He had almost nothing, only the bare essentials. If he was at home, I almost always found him folded up on his bed; I would set down the basket and say hello, and he'd reply with a nod. Other days he would come down to eat with us, to talk with Solomon about what he had to do. When he came in while we were reading, the fox told me to hide the book.

"Why?"

"Pipe down and do what I tell you!"

I asked him again in calmer circumstances.

"God isn't something for everybody," he said. "And definitely not for the stupid." He narrowed his eyes at me. "Are you stupid too?"

"No."

"There you go. So then treat them the way they deserve."

He started letting me hang around during his conversations with clients. If one of them happened to ask who I was, he told them I was his apprentice, and I felt proud. He gave me the wooden board he wrote on. He laid out all the terms and conditions of his agreements, which made it so he never failed to notice when someone was a day late or a seed short. He marked everything down using a thin stick that he dipped into a bowl of red ink. The ink was made from the blood of his chickens, or from crushed cherries, with snail slime stirred in. He had learned how to make it himself, as he had the boards he wrote on.

"I used to use my own blood, but then I lost too much weight," he said.

He made me start marking the things that he loaned. I had to draw a cross on the sack, or on the merchandise, so the client would know where the stuff had come from. On the board he noted the name and appearance of the client, if he was new or a regular. During their conversation he'd make them say where they lived, whether they had a family, and what all they owned. While I was learning to read the word of God, he would teach me, every now and then, how to make blank pages and write my own words, so that I could give him a hand once I had the knack of it. He told me I was being given a gift, and this was clear to me right from the start.

The old fox let me see the objects of man, which he'd been collecting for a lifetime; he showed me a leather casing into which they slipped their feet, some boards on which they drew, a stick that opened to form a hood, and various other little treasures. Solomon had figured out their functions for himself even if it took him days, as it had with the box. Since he had once been a man, he had to be capable of comprehending everything created by his own kind.

"Look here." He threw some pebbles on the table, which each time showed a different face.

"What are those for?"

"I don't know. Pipe down!"

*

At times the truth about things stopped me in the middle of whatever I was doing. If I was out walking in the snow, I would stand there in silence and stare at my footprints coming to meet me. The whitened forest seemed to have sunk into a deep sleep, as had a fair number of its inhabitants. And a deep feeling of lightness would come over me. I could feel how insignificant the trees were, and the grass, and the sky, and the earth. I could only be what I was, because that was the way God had willed it. My pausing like that was, finally, more like the current of a river than a rebellion. My consciousness changed nothing, I could feel it.

It was in one of those moments that I saw him coming from the trees. He climbed boldly up the hill with his back low against the cold and his big, bulky muzzle pointed at the door of the den, his mouth open to catch his breath. I had seen him only once before, but I recognized him immediately. I crept toward the den.

He was already talking to Solomon, who stood there listening with the board in his paw. He barked at him.

"I don't deal with vagabonds or with bandits, I just don't do it anymore," said the old fox. "If you've got something, you'd better come out with it now."

"I've got something," he said.

I inched toward them. When he saw me, he gave no sign of recognizing me. He took a little sack that he wore around his neck and dumped out the contents.

Solomon burst out laughing. "You want to sell me shards? Are you stupid?"

"They are things of man."

"It's broken. You'd better look for a hole before night. It's going to be a cold one."

I saw him stiffen, perhaps getting ready to attack the old fox, and at that moment I caught sight of the little fragments he had dumped out, all green and luminous. Cara and Louise had played with that thing, and in the end they'd broken it. My plunge into memory was interrupted by the arrival of Joel.

"So, are you leaving? Or will you be staying for dinner this evening?"

He gave in immediately, buckled, and murmured something.

"Just one egg…"

The old fox brushed aside the shards with one paw. "Get lost, you beggar!"

He threw the board at him. He backed away a bit, then puffed out his chest, at which point Joel stepped in between them and bared his teeth, driving him to the door in an instant.

"Have a good winter, my friend!" Solomon shouted at his back.

I ran out to see where he was going. He crossed the meadow in the opposite direction he'd come from. Mathias, my mother's love. He disappeared into the trees.

"What did he want?" I asked Solomon.

"What do you think? Food. I hate vagabonds, God knows how much." He picked the board up off the ground, having written nothing. "May the cold take him!"

I stared at one of the shards on the ground. I had no doubt, it was our mother's trinket. Instantly, the sight of it had set off an intolerable hum, which reverberated through me. My head was overwhelmed by curiosity, and my stomach churned. As time wore on, I bogged down in my ignorance, wanting more and more to be free of it.

7

The Things That Come Back

I TOSSED AND TURNED night after night, waking up in the dim light of my new window. When it snowed I watched the flakes flurrying in and thought about the things I had dreamed: Louise took me to the river and we wrestled, then she asked me to run away. Or I saw our mother's den in the spring when the grass was growing. When I opened my eyes I had a bitter sensation; the dreams felt more unreal and painful than ever, and when I thought about Mathias I could no longer sleep. During the day I tried not to think about it, but this wasn't easy and grew less so with time. I'd kept one of the shards that the marten had tried to sell to Solomon, and I ran it between my paws at night as I lay there sleepless, trying to fight off the nagging need to know what had happened. I relived my return, and the farewell I had said to my memories. In a way it was as if I'd only hidden them. Now they were moving around in the dark, inside of my sleep, and during the day I struggled to put them away as before.

It didn't take the old fox long to work out that something was wrong.

"You're distracted."

"No I'm not."

"Then tell me what you've just read."

He sighed, but he didn't lose his temper. His patient instruction filled me with guilt. I would have liked not to feel any of those things.

In the cold weather, fewer clients came around. By and large we did business with non-hibernators. Solomon started having me write on the board while he talked with them, and I made a real effort.

"Getting the hang of it? If he tries anything funny, he's as good as dead."

The old fox was pleased. I couldn't bring myself to respond in kind, even though deep down I was pleased too.

The next night, I dreamed of Louise again.

"Am I beautiful, Archy?"

"As beautiful as can be."

My sister led me to the little brook. She stared off into the distance, as she always did, distracted by her own thoughts. We twined together and lay there in silence, and she told me that she wanted to go away. I replied that I had already asked her to go away but she did not remember that.

"It's the season of mating," she said. She closed her eyes.

I woke up with a pounding heart. My head was still woozy from the sweetness of the dream, which as my vision readjusted slowly dissipated before turning into a sharp pang—a sign that even my mind was tired of tormenting itself. I got out of bed and went to the window. The moon was shining on the snow. It was at that moment I decided to give in to my inclinations.

"Go away? Have you lost your mind?"

Solomon had just sent Joel to do a job. I'd stood before him and told him my intentions. He looked back at me like I was a chicken ready for the slaughter.

"Only for a day, I'll come right back," I explained.

"I'll ask you again. Have you lost your mind?"

I shook my head no.

"And where would you like to go, in the cold, lame and weak as you are, you fool?" He came in close to me, breathing on my face.

I gulped. My paws were shaking. "I'm not running off, Solomon."

"You can swear you're not running off until you're blue in the face. Now get to work, so I forget the stupid stuff you come out with."

He turned his back on me. At which point a tremendous courage swept over me.

"I've got to go away."

The fox whirled around and dealt me a blow, which I avoided by taking a step back.

"Have you forgotten who's in charge here?" he shouted. "You're not going anywhere, you're my property!"

I stood my ground and answered his gaze. Tears welled in my eyes, but still I clung to my decision. Solomon was impressed for a moment, but then he lost his temper for real. He picked up the first thing he found—a basket of eggs—and threw it at me.

"Get your snout out of my sight, because I swear to God I'm going to kill you!"

He started to chase me and I jumped away, skittering all around the room dripping egg.

Solomon stopped. "Come over here, ass hair!" he said.

On the other side of the room, I was weeping. His looked at me scathingly, with hatred in his eyes.

"Don't make me repeat myself. I'm going to kill you, I swear."

There wasn't much I could do. I knew he was telling the truth.

Trembling, I approached him, my back low to the ground. He swatted me on the head with his paw, knocking me over.

"Where is it you want to go?" he said.

"To my mother's." I wept.

He swatted me with his other paw, harder. "You're not going anywhere. Got it?"

I nodded, in pain.

"Speak! Did you hear what I said?"

"Yes sir!"

He took me by the scruff and lifted me up, with unexpected strength, pushing me away.

"Get to work then!" he said. "And take a dip in the river to get that shit out of your head."

I went out into the snow, cold in my coat of yolks and whites.

"Stop crying!" he shouted. He stared at me from the doorway. "Make believe you're not a weakling!"

That day we didn't read. I cooked and we ate in silence, not exchanging a word. The old fox kept his muzzle shut, but there was no question he was irritated.

"Go to sleep."

That was how he got rid of me. Joel still hadn't come back. He must have been away for the night, off who knows where. In my bed I watched the darkness stirring with the wind, anything but sleepy. I got up and went to the window, where I kept the shard from Mathias.

64

Far away, in the snow, lay our mother's den. And Louise. I was unable to imagine her, to see her passing in the night before me. Beyond the darkness lay my uncertainty and ignorance. Sleep would only have magnified my desire, the desire to know what had happened. I went out through the window and made my way alone.

Beyond the meadow the snow wasn't so deep. The trees had gathered it in their branches, clearing the path and making it less difficult to follow; I could still remember the journey with Joel and was amazed to recognize some of the places we'd gone through. The darkness was frightening, and my swift-footed hobble filled the chilly silence. Even thinking about my decision terrified me, because I was sure I'd pay the price, Solomon's word.

To stiffen my resolve, I imagined that he would be moved to mercy when I came back instead of running off.

I hurried over the hill, went down too fast, and fell more than once. The faint roar of the Three Streams reached my ears as the water struggled to clear a path through the ice. I rested for a while under a fir tree. I was cold, and my breath came slow and sharp, scalding my throat. A noise from above made me jump. Darting away from the trunk, I caught sight of a large cat on a branch. In his mouth he held a mouse, still alive and giving out his last spasms. The cat observed me for a while.

"A dark and fearsome night," I mumbled.

I continued on my way, followed by his gaze.

My mother's den was submerged in snow. The two trees over the stone were ghastly and bare, the entrance almost completely covered. A small light glowed in the window, where Cara's silhouette was nowhere to be seen. I approached slowly, one step at a time, my heart urging me on toward the unknown.

"Who's there?" a voice erupted from within. It sounded anxious. The light went out in an instant.

I stood motionless, with every muscle tense.

"It's Archy," I said.

"Go away!"

I stayed a safe distance from the entrance.

"Excuse me, but doesn't Annette live here with her children?"

"There's no one with that name here, I told you to go away!"

I was silent for a while. I could hear movement inside the den.

"I don't want to hurt you," I said. "I just need some information."

"Get out of here! Or there will be trouble!" The voice sounded frightened.

"I beg you. Just one piece of information. Then I'll go away."

Again I heard movement. After a long while, from the little snow-covered entrance, the head of a big hare peeked out. He kept his eyes on me, not blinking once, and little clouds of breath flew fast from his nose.

"What do you want?" he spluttered.

"Information, please."

"Speak up."

"Don't beech martens live here?"

"Not anymore." The big hare kept his eyes on me, careful not to stick his head too far out. "I saw one of them, half blind."

I lit up. "Oh yes?"

From inside a higher-pitched voice murmured something. The big hare scuttled back for a moment to discuss. I waited for him to poke his head back out.

"She left us the den. My mate was pregnant, and we were cold." He thought for a moment. "A strange kindness," he concluded.

"Where did she go?"

"She asked us where to find the Great Stump. That was the one thing she wanted in return."

I tried to collect my thoughts.

"What's the Great Stump?"

"A place."

He explained how to get there, giving the same directions he had given the other marten. When he finished, still keeping his head out of danger, he waited for me to leave.

"Thanks," I said.

"Farewell," he said.

And so I went away from my mother's—the hare's—den. In the dark and the snow, it seemed to have nothing at all to do with the place I remembered.

It took me a long time to reach the Great Stump. During the journey my worries about my sister grew and grew. I was desperate to find out what had happened.

Finally, at the bottom of a cliff, in the middle of the woods, I saw the giant stump of a fallen tree, its roots protruding. Underneath was a hole, and in the shadows some traces of light. I hesitated before going in, filled with fear. In the presence of that place, all my instincts urged caution.

The air in there was heavy and acrid, drowning out any other scent. And the darkness was interrupted only by a few small lamps that were placed at the entrances of a series of tunnels. Discerning in the dim light the vague outline of a large animal, I froze with fear.

"Who's there?" I said.

He didn't answer me. He didn't move. I could hear his breathing, weak and unsteady, brushing against the walls of the room.

"Who are you?" I asked.

At that point he moved, and I was at the entrance in an instant, ready to flee. A weary voice came to me through the darkness. "Come in."

I remained silent. Carefully I leaned forward to see where he was. In the same place as before, I made out the eyes of a boar staring back into mine.

"Come in. I don't wish to do you any harm."

I inched forward. Now he could see me too.

"I'm looking for my sister."

The boar wheezed. "So look for her."

I edged in farther, and again we were face-to-face. His eyes remained fixed on the void.

"What is this place?" I asked.

"This is the Great Stump—the den that belongs to no one."

Only then did I realize he couldn't see me after all. He was old and fangless, curled up against the wall. He raised his snout to the ceiling and tore down a little root with his mouth.

"Whoever comes here has nowhere else to go," he murmured. "Or anything else to see."

And what I saw was precisely that. Beneath the tree there extended a series of tunnels and rooms. These were bare, poorly lit spaces, shared by animals of every species. Curled up in corners, they paid each other no mind, reaching out only to pluck roots from the ceil-

68

ing. A few turned to look at me, and others, seeing me as their predator, improvised a brief escape attempt. I too jumped back when I made out the shape of a dog in the darkness, but he did not come after me. All of them were old, crippled, sick, blind. Abandoned by others but still bound, like every animal, to life. As I observed those suffering faces, illuminating them with a lamp I'd taken at the entrance, I thought about God—about how cruel it was, to make us fight for something that will finally be taken from us. Even in their loneliness, in their exhaustion, their absence of appetite, they did not think they were going to die, and absurdly I envied them.

I could not find my sister. She was not in there, and no one who was in there had seen her. All hope of tracking down Louise and seeing her again began to fade inexorably. Emptiness stifled my fervor. A great sadness came over me.

"Who's there?" said the boar.

"Me again."

He grunted, then plucked a root from the ceiling. "Did you find the one you were looking for?"

"No."

A noise made me turn, and I saw a porcupine intent on changing the oil in the lamps. Speedily he vanished.

"Is it day or night?" the boar asked. "The birds don't sing much in this place."

"It's night."

He sighed. "Might as well sleep then. That way it will soon be tomorrow."

I stared at the entrance to the den for a while. By now I'd grown accustomed to the smell of the Great Stump, and it no longer bothered me. Without the impetus to go on and find Cara, I immediately felt exhausted. The feeling relieved me somehow of my fear and sadness. Sleep took care of the rest.

A loud dragging sound woke me with a start. Daylight beat into the den, and to my horror, I realized that a group of animals was heaving the boar outside. His eyes were still closed; his head no longer moved. Among those pushing him, I recognized several individuals I had seen in the lower rooms, and others I had never seen. I got to my feet and followed them.

Outside the entrance, scattered in the snow, a close-packed crowd of other animals had already gathered. Some were unwell, but many seemed healthy enough. They were waiting. As soon as the boar was completely clear of the Great Stump, they heaved him yet a little farther off. There was an agitated silence. And the moment they stopped pushing him, that silence became unbearable.

Suddenly they all lunged at the corpse. The air filled with cries and screams, snow flew and quickly crimsoned. In a free-for-all, they swarmed onto the body of the boar, trying to rip off pieces, crushing and biting each other in the process. The sight roused something in me. I remembered my hunger, my need to feed, and into the fray I lunged, wriggling in among the bodies, scratching, clawing, fighting off fear, inflamed by instinct. When I managed to grab something, I took it and put it in my mouth, got hit, and nearly flew sideways. Summoning all my strength, I got back to my feet, ignoring the pain in my paw. I bit everyone until they got out of my way and, before I knew it, I was there, on the boar.

Not since I'd killed the hen had I been so serene. No doubts, no questions. For a few moments the present was my whole world again, and outside of it there was nothing. I was an animal. I was happy.

Lifting my head from the boar's innards, covered in blood, in the squirming crowd, I spotted her. Missing the eye our mother had taken from her, she looked slightly mangier than I remembered.

"Cara!" I called.

She paused for a moment, saw me, and returned to the fray.

Before I could call to her again someone bit my tail and pulled me backward. I was soon engulfed by the others. As they pushed me aside, I kept shouting, euphorically: "God curse you! God curse you!"

And I laughed. Then they cast me out into the snow.

"What do you want?"

Cara moved cautiously up the slope of the cliff, and I followed her. With only one eye, she had to be careful where she put her paws, and every now and then she stumbled.

Her face was just as sad as I remembered.

"Where is Louise? Where is our mother?" I asked these questions with my heart in my mouth.

"They're dead, Archy."

I froze. She continued on her way, but turned back.

"Goodbye."

I felt a throbbing in my stomach, but I got the better of it. My eyes welled up, but not a single tear fell.

She had slipped into a den a little farther on, in the shelter of the cliff. I caught up with her and went in. I hit her with all the strength I could summon before she had time to turn around. And then I hit her again.

She started to scream, but I was on top of her immediately, pummeling her and holding my breath as my head pounded. The moment I stopped she crept to a corner of the room and cowered there. Only then did it dawn on me that she was living here alone, in a cramped little hole, with a tiny cot and a pinhole window. I noticed how sickly she looked, how gaunt, her rasping breath.

Two tears ran down my snout. "Take me to her," I said.

We picked our way back to our mother's den. The sun had risen in the sky, as pallid as could be. Although I hadn't asked, Cara began to talk about her life.

"When you're missing an eye you can't hunt. You can't run or stalk prey. The only place I can live is the Great Stump."

The Great Stump is the place where many animals choose to die. So it had always been, she knew. Everyone called it "the place of the long sleep." Blind, crippled, sick, and miserable animals populated it inside and out. The ones who died fed the ones who remained, eking out their existence. Sometimes in the winter jackals came, or wolves, and carried someone off, if they had no other way to survive. Other times they came to stay, and so the cycle kept going.

Cara talked about the others meeting their ends without including herself. As if she would be able to go on leading this existence forever, season after season. Once again, I felt envy.

Every morning she woke and went to wait with the others. When there was something to eat she charged into the fray; otherwise she wandered around looking for scraps or scavenging roots. Some days she did nothing but stand at her window, as in our mother's den. Her every word exuded profound resignation. But her speech was alive with energy, as if she'd been waiting a long time to tell these things.

"Louise got pregnant," she said, out of nowhere. "And our mother noticed."

Her tone was timorous now, perhaps out of fear I'd hit her again. I was hanging on her every word—so much so that I hadn't realized we were standing still.

"One morning she let us go out with her, when Mathias wasn't there. I went on pretending to be blind, so that she'd show me the way."

She had lowered her ears. Her voice was breaking.

"We stopped somewhere, and she told me not to move. That's when she grabbed Louise by the scruff and ran off with her. I heard her screaming and ran away."

My heart sank. Again I clenched my churning stomach.

"I went back home that night. There was no one around and everything was a mess, there was blood all over. Mathias must have killed her when he found out what happened."

I felt heavy. A stone at the bottom of a river. My eyes, not knowing where to look, fixed on the details of my sister's face. My silence made Cara breathe faster.

"Where is Louise?" I asked.

"Over there, I think."

And she pointed to a group of snow-covered stones near a slender tree. I trotted off, not saying a word to her. With every step I sank deeper into the riverbed. My nose clogged with snot, the cold stung my flesh, and tears cut my eyes.

Nothing.

There was only snow, nothing else.

I remember that feeling very well. Even today. The sudden sense of unreality that pervaded me in an instant, the foolish conviction that I'd been duped, that the whole story was a lie. I turned back to face Cara, but she had already gone, vanished, run away from my beatings, returned to her life of misery and solitude.

Then I saw a tuft of hair, a few steps farther on, sticking up out of the whiteness and swaying in the wind. I walked over, as if in a dream, and pushed away the snow.

In my mind it wasn't me digging at that moment. I was a kit again, in the spring, ready to play-fight. It was the same feeling I'd sensed fading at the sight of Mathias's face, and Solomon's face too.

I cleared the snow, and remembered that animals don't know how to lie.

"Hi there," I said.

At that moment all the things I'd seen, felt, or experienced came back—the before and the after, all at once. I saw her smoothing her fur and staring off into the distance, I heard her asking me if she was beautiful and not listening to the answer. I relived her scent and my wild dreams, the wish to run away together, and the season of mating, when she told me she loved me.

I remembered the toad looking at us from the far side of the brook. I remembered her face looking past me, her gaze elsewhere. Now that face was a mask of pain. The cold had pulled back the flesh, so that she gritted her teeth. Her eyes had frozen open, turned upward. Her belly had been ripped open—a wound that still spoke through the snow. Her paws, curled in on themselves, seemed to be searching for something nearby.

There she was in front of me. My Louise.

At that moment I felt as if I were nothing at all. I let myself go. I contemplated her and wept; I wept for my whole life.

When I was exhausted, ready to think about what I had to do next, I couldn't bring myself to do it. She would never go anywhere again. There was no more before, and no more after. I felt trapped. It was unjust. I wanted to forget, I could forget. And it was clear to me then that God was to blame. He was the one who willed it, he was the one playing with me. God was cruel to all of his creatures.

I cursed him, I asked him to smite me, but he didn't do anything.

No locusts arrived, no earthquakes or showers of blood. The day remained a day, with a pallid sun in a clear sky. And my life was not taken from me.

But along with the pain I felt inside, a need slowly began to make itself felt. The need to go back to Solomon's hill.

Joel spotted me the moment I emerged from the trees. He got to his feet but didn't come to meet me. From the top of his boulder he followed me with his eyes all the way to the hillside. In the old fox's den the lamps were lit, and a trickle of smoke poured skyward. Before I could reach the door, I saw him step outside with a stick.

I didn't try to run away, nor did I cower. He beat me hard, not saying a word, until I was flat on the ground with a bloodied mouth. Then he threw the stick aside and caught his breath.

"Get out of here," he said.

And went back into the den.

The sun, colored red, was taking its leave. I remained where I was, lying there in the snow, letting myself be overwhelmed by the pain. I hadn't pleaded with him and I hadn't wept. And that had made him beat me even harder.

A breeze began to blow, a very cold breeze, but I didn't care, I watched the first stars emerge from the darkness, in the winter silence, unafraid. I could have stayed there forever, watching the world grow old, like Louise.

Joel bit me hard on the scruff and carried me off. Inside the den, Solomon pointed at my room. I found myself back in my bed, with no trace of feeling left in my body. The old fox appeared at the door.

"Ass hair," he growled.

And he slammed the door shut.

8

The Rest of the Winter, *Tamam-shud*

As soon as I opened my eyes I was staggered by a sharp pain in my head. Then the pain spread through my whole body, leaving me gasping for breath.

Next to my bed was a cup of water, but I couldn't bring myself to move a muscle. Even turning my head gave me stabbing pains, as if I were trapped inside a blackberry patch. I decided to turn the other way, so as not to make myself any thirstier than I already was.

The light in the window was a midday light, the snow fell, and the wind blew. The memory of my brief journey soon conquered my thoughts, and I wished more than anything I could go back to sleep.

The old fox came into the room, dragging his chair behind him. His gaze immediately caught mine, but before paying me any mind he took his time getting comfortable. His eyes shot fire at me, restless and unwavering at the same time.

"Get to work," he said.

It was curious the way he sat there in anticipation, already knowing how I was going to reply. I said nothing, however.

"If you can't work I don't want you here, you're no good to me!" He began to cough.

"I can't get up, sir," I gasped.

The old fox shuddered, perhaps with the instinct to hit me. He looked at the cup beside my bed, threw it at me, and strode out.

Toward evening Joel came into the room. My first thought was that he was there to kill me. Instead, he left me a couple of eggs and a piece of chicken, along with another cup of water. He went out without saying a word.

The thing that surprised me most is that I wasn't afraid. I thought I was fine with dying. I ate what I could and wept.

"He hasn't broken anything but he has, perhaps, a slight fever. He should be feeling better in two weeks."

The next day Solomon had fetched a doctor, a fat beaver from who knows where. Throughout his visit I watched the old fox pacing back and forth across the room, impatient to hear about my condition.

The doctor, for his part, was terrified. Perhaps they hadn't fetched him in the gentlest possible manner.

"Two weeks?" The old fox glared at me fiercely.

"That's the time it will take, yes," the beaver stammered.

"It'd be quicker to kill him!"

"Well..."

Joel had appeared in the doorway. Immediately the doctor's fur stood on end.

"You could try giving him garlic and water. At least for the fever. Beyond that there's nothing to be done."

In that moment, as Solomon stood glaring at me, I could see all the annoyance he felt at the situation. He coughed.

"So he's fine?" The doctor nodded, and the old fox turned to Joel. "Give him a sack of wheat and take him back to where you got him from."

The beaver, his fur still bristling, rushed out of the room without a word of farewell.

We were left there alone.

"As God is my witness, as soon as you're better you're going to pay dearly," he muttered. He slammed the door behind him.

I didn't stir from the bed. Joel visited me morning and evening, bringing food and changing my bedpan, but Solomon never came. Through the door I could hear him going by, grumbling in his usual nervous way.

With every passing hour, I sank deeper into sadness and despair. My mind lunged at Louise's body lying in the snow like a thirsty man lunging at a poisonous spring. All my attempts to free myself from that image were in vain. I could just as easily have escaped the pain in my limbs. I had gone from being a prisoner of my thoughts to being a prisoner of my bed, and this filled me with rage.

I was angry with God because I couldn't feel otherwise. Perhaps if I hadn't known about him I wouldn't have complained so much, I would have accepted everything as it came, like a real animal. But knowing whose world this was, I had no choice but to see him as an enemy. It was instinctual.

After five days I was on the verge of madness. At night I couldn't sleep, and in the day I was persecuted by cruel little dreams. It was then that I noticed a stack of pages by the window, the pages that the old fox had taught me to make. I reached them by rolling myself over, trying to ignore the pain, but groaning with every roll I took.

I plucked a stalk of straw from my bed, the hardest stalk I could find, then bit my leg and dipped the straw in my blood. It worked. It wrote.

From that moment on I did nothing else. I stopped only when I heard Joel coming, or when I collapsed from weariness. I wrote about my journey and about Louise, about every sensation and emotion I experienced. One word led to another, each sentence was followed by the next. If at certain points I could not explain what I had in mind, I would try out new ways of thinking, I was talking with paper, I was looking at myself reflected in the mirror of my meanings. By the time I was finished, almost two weeks had gone by without my noticing. The pain in my body and the fever had subsided.

But that wasn't what surprised me. My rage had faded, along with my despair. My journey had become a memory, a terrible but ancient tale. Clutching the pages in my paw, I felt their weight and understood that things had changed forever. I had trapped my prison on paper.

Once more I was free—and sad.

When I woke it was still dark. I tore up the page where I cursed God, and then left my writing on the kitchen table. I took the bucket and went out to fetch the water as usual. The brook was almost frozen, and where I could still see the current I had to break through it with a stone. Certain movements still gave me a sharp pang, but it was nothing that I couldn't ignore.

Bit by bit I filled the big basin in the kitchen. Light began to rise behind the trees, preceding the sun. A few snowflakes floated down.

On my sixth trip I found the old fox in the kitchen, reading. I paused, but he told me to go on, with a brusque gesture of the paw, never taking his eyes off the pages. By the time I'd finished with the water, he was reading it from the start again.

"Eat," he muttered.

I lighted the fire and made breakfast, then went to feed the chickens. I took a few eggs, not all, so that others could hatch; I cleared the snow from the entrance to the coop.

Solomon had set my story down. He watched me come in and put the eggs away. When I was done, I just stood there facing him. In his angry face, I made out a hint of gentleness and pride.

"Do you know what love is?" he said.

I had never given it any thought. It was always just a feeling, an instinct. I told him so.

"No, that isn't love," he said. "And it isn't your pining for that sister of yours either. Those are animal things. Fucking, getting stuck on a scent, wrapping your bodies around each other—those things are for idiots." He coughed. One of his paws gripped the table. "The only real Love is love of God. Anything else is destined to die with us."

I believed he was right, and Louise's disfigured face again passed before my eyes.

The old fox picked up the pages with his paws. "There is Love here, between the lines. It can't be read, but it makes itself felt."

He sat there spellbound for a few moments, then shook himself.

"Get back to work!" he growled.

81

I left the kitchen, quick. Repeating to myself that my relationship with Louise was a futile thing didn't lift my spirits. Realizing that, for a futile thing, I'd stopped loving God, however, gave me no small amount of courage.

Contrary to what he had promised, Solomon didn't punish me. I continued to slave away for a few days, and then he went back to teaching me and treating me as his assistant. He realized that I'd changed, that I'd stopped weeping and lowering my eyes when he glowered.

"What is this, are you done being a weakling?"

He raised his paw and I dodged him. It was enough to satisfy him.

"God destroyed Sodom and Gomorrah," I read.

"Yes. Why?"

"Because they rebelled against God."

"Exactly. See that you don't meet the same fate."

That evening I saw that he was pensive and I couldn't understand why. I didn't ask, of course—that would only irritate him. He stood by the fire, wrapped in a blanket, munching chestnuts left over from the fall and coughing now and then.

"I came down with something from beating you," he said. "Let's hope the spring comes soon."

The weather was so punishingly cold that there were days now when no clients came. The old fox had me move the chickens out of the coop to keep them from freezing to death. He said to put them in my room, as he'd always done during the harshest winters. Then he told me to push my bed into the kitchen. He even called Joel down from his pallet on the boulder to take up residence in the entryway. For many nights we slept together under the same roof.

This pleased me. There was great power in it: a silent struggle against the sulking heavens, and against God himself. Solomon often fell asleep in the kitchen by the fire, right next to me. He talked in his sleep, but often I took him to be awake and called out to him.

"What's that?"

"Did I say something?"

"No."

He stood up, stoop-backed, and hobbled to his room. He was old.

Now that we no longer went outside, we read all day. The old fox made me rewrite certain passages—the more difficult ones—using different words.

"Now they're comprehensible," he said with satisfaction.

"Does God allow these things to be rewritten?" I asked.

He thought it over. "No." He tore up the pages and threw them in the fire.

The moon followed the sun, and vice versa, many times. As one page followed another, to the end of the book. My master closed it gently, stroking it with his paw.

"Now you know the word of God, my father. The only truth about the world."

He was moved. In truth I had learned all these stories with a sense of reluctance, still staggered by how cruel God was. All the parts about forgiveness, about his goodness, never made me forget what he'd done to me or the hatred I felt for him.

"There's no need to fear, if you're on his side he's on your side," the old fox said, coughing.

Why had he inflicted this pain on me? Why wasn't I a man?

83

Hadn't I sought him, hadn't I been on his side? Why had he killed Louise?

I thought these things but said nothing. Solomon would not have understood. He would have beaten me like the Hebrews beat the infidels.

"*Tamam-shud*," he said. "It is done."

Then he came up to me and wrapped me in an embrace. I was caught by surprise and didn't know what to do. I let him clasp me tight, gripping my fur without hurting me, as calm as could be. I had never seen him so unguarded. I returned his embrace.

That was the moment in which I found him closest to God by far, the same moment in which I could not have been more distant from him.

He let go of me and smiled, then looked into the distance. And he stood up abruptly, moving toward the window.

"Ah! Here comes his benevolence now! Praise be!" he shouted, turning back to me.

I went to join him. "What's going on?"

"Do you see those flowers?" He pointed to a little far-off clump of seedlings sticking up out of the snow. "Winter's at an end."

9

The Second Book

IN JUST UNDER A WEEK the snow began to melt. A few trees had already put out their first buds, and the hill was stained a faint green. All those waking from hibernation rushed out to buy and borrow, urged on by their enormous hunger. Solomon negotiated the deals, I wrote down the details, and Joel kept everyone in check. Once he had to kill a cat who had pounced on a gerbil.

"Who wants him?" the old fox shouted. And the cat got bought up too.

The hens went back into the coop and I regained my room.

"What is it, aren't you pleased?"

"Yes."

"Doesn't seem like it."

Solomon couldn't accept that I'd grown hard-nosed; he couldn't wrap his head around it. Perhaps he was unable to imagine the unsophisticated way I experienced things, or perhaps he liked playing the part of God.

In the meantime, between one task and the next, I had begun to take an interest in the woods, wanting to discover the places hidden among the trees. Once spring arrived, Joel would stay out for days on end and come back from who knows where, wounded sometimes, or covered in dirt, or with someone in his jaws. I began to wish I could go with him and see what he saw.

"Brunhilde, female stoat, sack of wheat. You got that down?"

"Yes."

The old fox talked with the client in a quick, aggressive manner to put the fear into her.

"Trade for two chickens, one lays eggs, the other doesn't, four days from today. Good?"

"Yes."

The stoat plucked out a lock of her hair. Solomon took it and gave it to me and I put it next to what I'd written. He gave me a sack of wheat, and she went away down the hill, not looking back.

"Four days," he shouted, and was overcome by a coughing fit. "Miserable animals."

Things were going well for us. We were glutted with food. We ate three meals a day.

Solomon always used to thank God, then grab his paunch and thank himself. He'd laugh.

"You come to your senses yet, you idiot?" he'd say to me. "Laugh, laugh—there's no other cure in the world."

I'd grown bigger, more muscular. I still limped, but I could keep up a good pace. The new season reinvigorated my instincts. My head vibrated furiously in response to such scents. At last I plucked up my courage.

"I want to go with Joel and get to know the woods."

The old fox was sitting in his chair, watching the sunset.

"Be careful you don't make me angry," he said.

"I could be helpful. I could write about the places I see."

"May God strike you dead!" he shouted, then started to cough. He leaned back. "Don't make me get out of this chair. I'm thinking."

He woke me up in the middle of the night. He was agitated, feverish, his eyes zigzagging around the room.

"Come into the kitchen," he told me.

He had me sit down at the table, by the light of a candle. He took out a book I had never seen before, made from the same paper we used. He set it down in front of me carefully, like a precious object. Fighting off sleep, I began to leaf through the pages.

"Be careful with it, you idiot!" he hissed.

From top to bottom, it was filled with words, sometimes written in different colors, until the pages turned blank.

"Is this God?" I asked, still groggy.

"No. This is me." He stroked the book reverently. The shimmer of the candle in his eyes illuminated his muzzle. He got to his feet, left the kitchen, and came back with another book, wonderfully made, almost as perfect as the Bible. He set it under my nose, I opened it, and I saw that it was completely blank.

"I want you to write about me, as you know how to do, with Love."

I looked at him, perplexed. He slid one book beside the other.

"I want you to rewrite my life, to bring it closer to God."

I yawned. "Now?"

The smile died on his lips, as quick as a flash.

"Now and for as long as it takes. Let's get started."

Under the sun I slaved away. In the dark before dawn, I was awoken to get back to writing. The old fox was as excited as a pup, and he shook me from sleep with the strength of a much younger animal. I became accustomed to hearing the sound of his cough behind the door whenever he was coming to fetch me. I'd open my eyes, but I couldn't bring myself to get up.

"'I am the only child of my mother, Celine,'" I read.

He stopped my paw. "'I am a child of God, born a fox to Celine, by his will.' Write it."

He changed so many things. He sneaked in God in wherever he could manage it. Most of his deeds and adventures were transformed into missions undertaken on behalf of the one and only truth. Each murder, theft, and misdeed became an episode in his search for the light.

The old fox dictated to me with his eyes turned toward the ceiling, polluting his memories with pious morals, and grunting with satisfaction at each lie he concocted as if it were the truth of things. At the time I thought he was crazy, but today I can say with certainty that he was attempting to save himself; he was doing all he could to get to Heaven.

With my paw I wrote, but with my eyes I lapped up the story of his life, joining in his adventures as a bandit, passages that enthralled and transported me, igniting my imagination as the word of God had never done. He spoke of the world as it was, its infinite cruelty, death, the pains that each and all must suffer. After a while I started waking up before he did. I couldn't wait to go on. I forgot all about spring and the forest.

"'I steal hens with Victor and we kill the others for fun.' Wait. 'We took one hen for ourselves and sacrificed the rest to the Lord.' Put it down like that."

Parts were missing. The narrative broke off abruptly at certain points where the pages had been torn out. Solomon told me not to pay them any mind, but I could see that the book had been tampered with, because some stories were incomplete. Some very curious stories.

He had traveled far and wide. He had met with bears, wolves, the king of the stags—animals never seen in these parts. He'd picked up some companions, bandits with whom he formed a band that shared rules and raids. True to his nature, he had known hunger, danger, and a vagabond life, never questioning the way he behaved. He made me take out all those stories, but I couldn't help but envy him. At dawn on a clear, calm day, I put down my pen and looked him in the eye.

"Solomon, I want to see the woods. I want to see God's creation."

The old fox bristled, but he didn't lose his temper. With a little snort he regained his composure.

"You can't, you're a fool and a cripple. You want other reasons?"

I folded my paws. "Then I'm not going to write another word, Solomon," I said.

A shiver ran down my spine because I'd said too much, I knew it. With a lightning-quick gesture he struck me in the face, knocking me to the ground.

"Not going to write?" he shouted. "That's a good one. I'll cut those paws off and let's see what kind of joker you are." He threw the new book back at me. "Every season it's something with you! But you're not free, you're my property, you shit!"

Before he could catch his breath to say another word, I pounced with all the strength I had. We fell to the ground in a heap and rolled around the kitchen, making a racket. I didn't bite him, and he didn't try to bite me; perhaps the shock I'd given him made him think twice. He grabbed me by the ear and yanked it hard, I had him pinned down with one paw and with the other I was squeezing his nose.

"Bastard! Bastard!" I shouted. I'd wanted to say that for a long time. Tears sprang to my eyes.

Joel barged into the kitchen, tossing me aside with one paw. I bounced against the wall and, a moment later, found myself face-to-face with his open jaws.

"Enough! Enough!" the old fox shouted.

The dog shoved me against the wall again and went on growling. Solomon got up, coughing, and hurried to hide the books. With his fur all bristling, he looked a terror, and there was a murderous expression in his eyes.

"What are you doing here?" he growled.

Joel turned to him. "I heard noises."

"Go listen to the birds, nobody called you!"

The dog, perplexed, let me go.

"Come on, shoo! Get out of here!"

The old fox gave me a look. I thought he would leap onto the table, pounce, and kill me then and there. Instead he set the books on the table as before, picked up the pen, and righted the color cup. He turned and stared at me.

"Write," he said.

His spoke so sharply that I shook with worry. The voice of reason implored me to return to my seat as if nothing had happened. But I'd seen it all too many times by now.

"No."

The old fox hurled the books aside, along with the inkwell and the pen, and flipped over the table and chairs. But he didn't come at me. Not a single step. Suddenly he was overcome by a fit of coughing, and he coughed so hard that, bent double, he collapsed on the ground beside me. It dawned on me that he was weeping.

"Write, I beg you," he murmured.

I felt sorry for him. Without realizing it, two tears ran down my snout too. Fear slipping away?

"No."

10

All That Is Just

THE FIRST OPPORTUNITY to present itself was the unpaid debt of a pig named David. Pigs are slow and stupid, and the old fox thought there wasn't much danger there. Joel was waiting outside, sitting on the ground. Solomon gave him a sack with three apples, two for me and one for him. Scornful, irritable, anxious, he looked at us.

"Keep him safe or you're dead," he declared.

The dog nodded, turned, and trotted downhill. I followed. Three times I turned back to see the old fox still there, on his hind legs, watching us disappear into the trees. What was it, I wondered, that bound him to me? Was it God, or writing, or affection? We had left off just past the midpoint of his book. We'd resume when I returned.

I was excited. In the depths of the woods everything was unknown, mysterious, and disquieting again. God might be all around us, but I had left him behind with the old fox on the hill. My sadness, however, I always had with me, even if, for the time being, it had lifted a little.

We were headed toward the far side of the Three Streams, to a narrow clearing wedged in between the trees, a stone's throw from a pond. Joel knew the way, and without betraying his natural silence he led me there. Once during our journey he suddenly came to a halt, telling me to do the same.

"What is it?" I whispered, on edge.

He sniffed the air, pointed, and listened, all his muscles taut. I held my breath, my heart beating faster.

"It's a long way off," he said. He relaxed. "Let's keep going."

Later I learned that the pigs inhabited the clearing only in summer and spring. The pig families spent their winters apart and in a den of their own, surviving as best they could. In the beginning it had been otherwise, but then overcrowding beset them, and a great pestilence. Oaks surrounded the clearing and dropped their acorns in the fall. The pond that the clearing overlooked was shallow and muddy and perpetually cool.

Each family had its own den, but the outside space was held in common, and there no one sought to take advantage of his neighbor.

The pigs seemed to me neither slow nor stupid. Like boars, they had short fur, but their tusks were less prominent and they weren't so heavily built. When they saw us coming, they all ran to hide, both the males and the females, the mothers and the young. We were left there alone, in the middle of the clearing.

After a little while, from a long way off, a big sow came to meet us, followed by two powerful-looking males. She must have been the chieftain of the families, the most venerable member. Pigs put the females in charge of everything.

"Dog!" she shouted. "Your master has no business here! Take your companion and go back home!"

As she approached, I realized that, all around us, other pigs were springing up from their dens. Though they kept their distance, they were prepared to charge. Joel paid no heed. He kept his eyes on the big sow, who was close enough to conduct a normal conversation.

"Get out of here," she said.

"Who are you? Where's Giuditta?" the dog replied.

The other pigs had formed a circle around us and were quaking with nervous tension. I was restless myself and kept turning, turning, in all directions.

"Giuditta has had her day. I'm in charge here, and what I say is that we won't be doing business and other animals have no place here. Get out or the joke's on you. We aren't afraid."

Joel ignored the threat.

"We're looking for David, who contracted a debt last summer with Solomon the lender," he said.

The big sow grunted, and I shuddered. I could feel it in my bones. Something was about to happen.

"The man took David last winter. He's not far off, but now he lives it up behind a silver thread, well fed and watered and never moving a muscle."

All the pigs murmured, as if they knew the story and envied him.

"Someone has to pay," said Joel.

The big sow beat her hoof against the ground.

"Get out of here!" she said again.

And so, as I anticipated, at the slightest irritation, after a few brusque words, the pigs gave vent to their fury.

Instantly, three of them were on us. With one paw Joel brushed me aside, pushing away the first, dodging the second, and ripping the ear of the third clean off. Screaming dreadfully, gushing blood, the pig leapt desperately away. Hearing his scream, the others followed suit. In no time at all they disappeared underground. We were alone again.

"Take this. Keep your eyes peeled."

He gave me the sack of apples and hurried off toward one of the dens. Finding an opening, he stuck in his muzzle, and the rest of his body quickly followed. There wasn't a living soul left in the clearing except me, the sack of apples in my paws. I kept looking around so as not to be caught off guard, my heart pounding. From underground I could hear screams, but it was impossible to tell where they were coming from.

I inched over toward the den into which Joel had disappeared, but as soon as I saw the opening a pair of pigs bolted out. I screamed, thinking they were attacking, but they dodged me with a leap, terrified and bent on their escape. Then another bolted out. I began to make noises, threatening to bite, and he squealed at the top of his lungs, kicking away across the clearing. I was beside myself with joy. From the opening I heard more screams and got ready for the next batch, baring my teeth in excitement. But I found myself confronted with the largest pig I'd even seen. He hurtled out at top speed, covered in blood, with his mean pugnacious eyes pointed right at me. My euphoria drained away, pronto; out of instinct, I threw the sack of apples at him and took off running as fast as I could. From the corner of my eye I could see him gaining on me, his breath heavy, his wounds glistening, but in the end he galloped off to the side. I stopped. Joel had emerged from a hole in the distance with a piglet in his mouth who was screaming as if to wake the dead. Only then did I see that his larger kin had also wriggled out and were running after him. The dog dodged a couple of them and ran in a long, curved line, dragging them behind him and heading straight for me. In his eyes I clearly read the word "Run," and I did. I chose the point nearest to the woods and hurled myself at it as hard as I could, trying not to put too much weight on my aching leg as the turbulence at my tail came closer and closer. When Joel caught up with me, he used his head to toss me aside and throw me on top of him with incredible strength. While he was at it, he almost let the pig escape from his mouth, but he grabbed him on the fly, biting into his fur while I held on to Joel's, to keep from falling and being trampled by our pursuers. I rode the dog's back fast across the clearing, toward the trees. Behind us the pigs were desperate to keep up: they were terrifying to behold, ragged as they were, with their eyes so full of pain and hatred. Our prisoner kept on screaming for help, with Joel's breath hot on his neck. Then I saw the oaks blotting out the sun, the air became cooler and more intense; we began zigzagging among the trees and bushes. Even so someone kept trying to follow us, but soon gave up; we were too far ahead. Before long only their screams pursued us, filtered through the branches of the forest.

"I'm over here! I'm over here!" our prisoner cried.

I was elated.

"Pipe down, ass hair!" I shouted at him.

We came to a halt in a quiet place. Joel told me to make a tether out of whatever I could find, and I made do with a creeper. The pig's neck was punctured in several places, and he squealed in pain when I tied him up.

He had gone on calling to his companions until the dog had

beaten him. After that he'd started murmuring "Cowards, cowards," weeping all the while.

I had lost the sack of apples, and now hunger had us in its grasp. There was no reproof, however. Joel was too busy catching his breath.

"Do you know David?" he said at last.

Our prisoner pricked up his ears. "Yes."

"Where is he?"

"The man took him, last winter."

"So he's dead."

"No, I've seen him, he's in a pen, alive."

Joel stood there thinking for a moment. "If he isn't there, we'll kill you."

"I can take you to him, I can take you right to him."

"Too dangerous."

The young pig began to tremble and weep. "No, no, I can take you there, there's only the one man, the pen is small, and the dog is old," he sobbed.

"Let's go there, Joel," I said.

I had never seen a real man, a child of God. Curiosity suddenly boiled in my brain.

"No," said the dog.

"It isn't far, I can take you, I can take you." The young pig had pissed himself. His bright, vivid eyes clung desperately to my muzzle.

"Let's go there and get David," I said.

"I can take you, I can take you," the pig kept saying.

Joel was thinking things over. He didn't want to put me in danger and incur the old fox's wrath. Even though Joel could easily have killed Solomon, Solomon's threats had tremendous power over him. He feared him like a lightning storm. On the other hand there was a debt that remained unpaid, and an animal who was getting away with it.

"Let's go see what we can see," I said.

"Yes, yes, I can take you."

Our prisoner had broken into a smile, a sort of terrified exultation. When he moved he pulled on the tether, choking on a sob, paying no attention to his wounds or the blood that poured from them.

"This way, this way."

At the foot of a wooded hill was the den of the man. It was big and rose up from the earth like a leafless tree, separated from the earth. We observed it from a wheat field, hidden among the blades, waiting for the sun to finish setting. In the moments before we went in I became very frightened; the man was there looking back at us, and Joel hadn't noticed.

"It's not the man," he whispered. "It's only a shadow, to scare away the birds."

The young pig pointed to a pen a few steps from the den. Inside the pen were two pigs, one fatter than the other, lying side by side.

"There he is, he's the smaller one."

The other pig was a pregnant sow. She was resting her snout serenely on David's back. It was clear that she was expecting children; they had been busy in that pen. And there wasn't much else to occupy them; apart from the tub of water in the corner, they lived on a barren patch of ground, like Solomon's chickens.

Their peaceful sleep made an impression on me. I couldn't say whether it was a horrible way to live or not, whether being confined inside a fence was comforting or degrading. From where I stood, I pitied them, like the others; yet their faces suggested that they might pity us.

The man emerged from his den with a dog. They were both old, with long hair and weary eyes. The pigs woke up and watched them walk into the pen, showing no fear of them. The man had a sack in his hand and was holding it upside down in front of him. The pigs began to eat what he dropped.

Apart from his age, he was similar to the figures I'd seen on the box and on Solomon's colored boards; he was covered in fabrics and had no pelt, only some white fur growing on his muzzle. So that was what a child of God, a saved soul, looked like.

From the door of the burrow another man emerged. Much younger and slenderer. A female. She appeared in the doorway and spoke to him in the language of the Bible, a few quick words I understood with some difficulty. She told him to come back in.

The old man closed the fence and turned around, wiped his back paws off outside the door, then patted the dog and let her loose. She walked around the den and curled up by the door.

"Let's wait a little longer," said Joel.

We waited long enough to let the fear subside.

The night came down. The lights in the burrow went out, and there was no longer any noise except the night. Joel stood up from his hiding place and tugged at our prisoner.

He wasn't doing too well; he looked spent, and his breath was coming fast and shallow. The wounds on his neck had dried. Now they were swollen, shining holes that reflected the light of the moon.

"You lure him to the edge of the pen," Joel said to him.

"Yes, all right, all right."

"Make up an excuse, tell him you're wounded, get him to stick his neck out."

"I will."

"Your life is on the line."

Joel gave me the tether to hold. The young pig was trembling again.

"Take him to that piece of the fence, then hide on the ground, in the grass. And don't let go," he said.

I nodded and stood up too.

"Don't make a sound."

The dog went first and hid. I watched him move and heard nothing but the rustling grass. Trying to do likewise, I marched the prisoner to the spot Joel had indicated. As we got closer to the fence, with my heart in my throat, I looked around for a place to hide. The shapes of the two pigs were visible in the darkness. We were there. Quickly I crouched down in the grass and let the tether go slack; the prisoner noticed and started, but I gave it a tug to let him know I still had a hold on him.

I couldn't see where the dog had taken cover. The young pig trembled and kept looking where I was hiding until I raised my head and stared him down.

"Get on with it," I whispered.

"David," he called out softly. "David."

The shapes in the pen shook themselves.

"Who's there?" The voice that spoke was thick with sleep.

"Help me, David," the prisoner said.

One of the two shapes rose to its feet.

"Who is it, David?" said the sow.

"I don't know. Who are you?"

The pig was approaching the fence. I could see him more clearly now, as he inched forward, straining his eyes, sticking out his snout to catch the scent.

"It's Ciro, David. I'm wounded."

David edged closer, until he could see who it was.

"What are you doing here? Are you alone?" he said.

The prisoner hesitated. I saw his eyes strain in my direction, and an overwhelming shudder ran down the whole length of my tail.

"I'm wounded, David. Look." He showed him the tether around his neck, and the holes. "I can't get it off, help me."

David took another step and was up against the fence.

"Who is it, David?" the sow repeated. There was worry in her voice now.

"I know him, he's my cousin," he said. "What are you doing here?"

"Help me." The prisoner offered him his neck, careful not to get too close, so that he had to poke his head through. "Get it off me."

David stood there in silence, perplexed, not budging from the spot.

"A cousin of yours?" The sow got to her feet and came to join him.

"Get it off me," the prisoner repeated.

"What does he want? He's wounded?" The sow came closer.

"Get this thing off me."

"I can't reach, come closer," said the sow.

"Are you alone?" David said again.

"Here we go, I've got it."

Joel bolted in out of nowhere. He pushed the prisoner aside and at full speed fastened his jaws to the sow's throat, stopping only by dint of the bite. She let out a dreadful scream, her eyes went wide, and she tried to get back on her feet but couldn't run away. David, surprised, leapt into the air and screamed in turn. Joel squeezed harder and was soon drenched in blood black as pitch, the color of the night. The sow screamed again, but the sound died out into a desperate gurgle, a violent convulsion. David tried to pull her back into the pen, screaming for help. The dog managed to bite her again and got a better grip, but by now her throat was agape and her eyes were unblinking. The smell of the blood had reached my nostrils, and with an effort I suppressed my instinct to attack, not wanting to complicate matters for Joel.

"Who's there? Who's there?"

The man's dog had begun to howl. Hearing her, the prisoner made a break for it; he pulled with all his strength on the tether, which pulled me along with it, dragging me out of my hiding place, into the yard.

I braced my feet against the ground, summoning my strength. The young pig choked on the tether and stopped running. The man's den was all lit up, and my fur stood on end. Joel came toward us, spitting out a piece of flesh.

"Run! Run!"

All three of us ran toward the wheat field.

David's scream tore through the night, accompanied by the howling of the dog.

"Who's there? Who's there?"

"Don't stop!" said Joel.

A loud clap of thunder exploded behind us, followed by a whistle. Then we were in the thick of the wheat field, safe.

*

We came to a halt not too far away, once the forest had covered our tracks. I smiled breathlessly, my whole body radiant with the euphoria of someone whose life has just been hanging by a thread. It had been a bandit's adventure, a bona fide raid, and it reminded me of Solomon's book.

"Now set me free," the young pig said.

He was panting. By running he'd reopened his wounds. Joel took me aside for a moment.

"Kill him," he told me.

I nodded. The young pig was quick to read my look, the step with which I returned to him, the way I was holding on to the tether. He retreated immediately, trying to keep his distance from me, doing further damage to his neck.

"I didn't rebel, you've got to free me!" he shouted.

The prisoner began to weep and threw himself on the ground, spluttering pleas I no longer remember.

"I didn't rebel, I didn't rebel."

I leapt at him, holding the tether taut and choking him. He kicked out as best he could, striking at my face, keeping me at a distance.

"No! No!" he screamed, then sobbed as I pulled.

I had no hesitation. I did not ask myself any questions or feel any pity. Without feeling anything, I watched death take possession of his eyes and enter his thoughts. The young pig was dying and knew it now; he could sense it. When I got too tired to go on struggling, I leapt at his throat and bit him. I tasted the blood on my tongue and felt him jerk.

"No, no," he said again, for the last time.

His eyes went wide, then emptied and stared off into the distance. His breathing stopped, while mine went on quite rapidly. I had killed him and felt no remorse, he had asked for his freedom and now he was dead, it was unjust but it didn't matter; God was cruel.

We ate him, leaving only the head. Joel pointed down at the body. "Who's this?"

I didn't have to think. "David."

"Exactly."

11

Anja

AFTER THAT FIRST ADVENTURE, others followed. From time to time, whenever a simple task presented itself, the old fox would let me go with Joel and get to know the forest. He didn't send me very far, but events often carried us a bit farther than anticipated, as in the case of David.

I became adroit at handling dangerous situations and I always followed Joel's orders when he gave them. On a few occasions, when violence didn't do the trick, he even had me do the talking. My companion in adventure hardly ever spoke. He showed me with gestures. I never knew if he was sad or happy or even anxious; no matter what was happening, his face remained almost entirely impassive. I wondered how he perceived the world, whether he experienced emotions or desires, if he ever felt the need to weep. He never backed down from anything, completed his missions without exception, and feared nothing apart from our common master. I discovered that, in some areas, Solomon was known as "the fox with the long memory," which made me think again about the power of writing and its immunity to time. I continued to transcribe his book as he went on dictating new sentences, altering his own story.

"Solomon, there's a piece missing here."

Right at the end of the page a word broke off, disappearing into nothing. Then the narrative resumed with another word, a different subject.

"Keep going."

"But there's a piece missing."

"And you can keep right on going."

He coughed. That hollow hack of his had never gone away. He had been dragging it around with him all through the spring. In the evenings he'd sit outside in his chair and watch the sunset. I would bring him the first grapes or an apple off the tree; if I'd finished with my chores I'd sit down next to him.

"The world is very beautiful," he said once. "The grass, the water, the trees, the air—beautiful." He took a deep breath.

"Maybe it's beautiful because there's only one," I offered.

The old fox turned and gave me a look of irritation. "This is how I would have made it if I were him." He pointed skyward. "We have similar tastes."

"Indeed."

During the day the clients came and went. I transcribed the deals on the board, marking the goods and noting down details as relayed to me by Solomon. I didn't dislike the work, but all the time I was waiting to take off again. When I was stuck in the den for too long, sadness would catch up with me: it would creep out of the forest, where I'd shaken it off the last time, and then there was no cure but to wander.

One evening in early summer we found ourselves confronted with a pair of beech martens. I didn't notice them at first because

I was busy writing, but the moment I looked up I dropped the board. Hiding shyly, behind a sturdy-looking male with a flattened muzzle, was the most beautiful creature I had ever seen. She looked back at me with eyes like jewels, large and unwavering.

I flushed and stood there breathless, giddy, feeling wobbly yet stiff.

"Are your paws too heavy for you? Pick it up!"

The old fox's voice jolted me back to reality. I looked away, picked up the board, and immediately turned to face her again. She was still staring at me, without any embarrassment, rousing my senses and stirring something deep inside. I perceived right away it was instinct, rising from below, the impulse to make her mine, right there in front of the others, without fear or doubt, heaven or earth, the world or God, because I was nowhere if I was not with her.

I managed to swallow the passion rising in my throat, to suppress it with a shiver, to lower my gaze. And I was crushed by sadness. I no longer felt like an animal; I had traded my instincts for questions and doubts, for the exercise of reason and the falsification of my nature. Solomon would have said it was a stupid feeling, a fictitious love, and I was giving that some consideration now. I was also considering God, the curse of having found him, and Louise.

"Write!"

I shook myself.

"Hector, marten, three hens."

"Yes."

I raised my head and found she was still staring at me.

"Lives in the woods to the south, near the Sunken Rock."

My paw shaking, I was writing everything down wrong.

"Trade for six sacks of carrots in two days' time, agreed?"

"Agreed."

The old fox snatched the board away from me and reread the record of the trade.

"Are you rich?" he said.

The marten called Hector did not seem to be familiar with the term.

"What if I gave you four hens in exchange for ten sacks of carrots?"

"Sounds good to me."

Solomon became suspicious. He stared daggers at him, as he would have at a bandit. He handed the board back to me.

"How about this? I'll give you one hen now and then you bring me three sacks of carrots. If you bring them, I'll give you the others, and I'll send someone to pick up the rest of the sacks."

Hector thought it over and stood there, bewildered. "We need three hens," he muttered.

"Either we do it like I say or you don't get any. Done deal?"

I had gone back to staring at her. When she noticed, she stared right back. Her unsustainable gaze began to fill me again, and the world faded around her. My eyes pleaded with me to turn them somewhere else, to blind them or hide them, but I preferred to let them linger. I preferred to feel defenseless.

The old fox sent me to fetch a chicken, and I hurried without delay to the coop. I grabbed the first hen who happened past and was back in no time, trying to limp as little as possible.

"In two days' time, three sacks of carrots, got it? No funny stuff, because we'll find you," said Solomon.

"Here you go." I handed over the hen. I tried to breathe in her scent, but she was too far away, and the odor of the male was overpowering.

The old fox eyed them, still not satisfied. "Are you a family?"

"This is my sister Anja."

"Whose children are you?"

"Our father is Sasha the Great."

The old fox reflected. "Never heard of him. In two days' time, three sacks of carrots."

Anja.

I remember that I thought of nothing else as I watched her descend the hill and dive into the trees. And I thought of nothing else afterward, for the rest of the day. My doubts had taken a step back and it was plain as day: Anja was not a foolish thing or a fictitious feeling; Anja was something that I wanted at any cost.

The next morning Hector returned without her, accompanied by another male. They brought four heavy sacks of carrots. The old fox saw them coming through the kitchen window while we were making breakfast.

"I told you they were bandits," he said.

He had them put the sacks by the door of the den and checked their contents. While the two martens took their ease he sent me to fetch three chickens, telling me to make sure to choose ones that didn't lay eggs. When I got back Joel was there too, studying the strangers in silence. I tied the legs of the three chickens with a string, then handed them to Solomon as they thrashed about.

"You still owe us six sacks," he said with a cough. He pointed at me and Joel. "They'll go with you and carry the other three back here, all right?"

The two martens said it was all right by them. I was thrilled. I was going to see Anja. The old fox passed the hens to Joel and shot him a warning look, the same look he gave me when I went off into the woods. The dog gestured subtly with his head. A little while later the hill was behind us.

The two martens led the way, Joel was in the middle, and I brought up the rear. The strangers soon saw I couldn't move too quickly and slowed their pace without a word from anyone. We hardly talked at all; on the paths, it was best to be quiet, keep an eye out for danger, but still I managed to learn that the other marten was called Biko. They were bigger than I was, torn and scarred from fighting, and their eyes were harder than mine. They didn't seem to get along. In fact the only time I saw them in agreement was at the stream where we stopped to drink. They came over and told us that we were going too slow. They looked at me nastily, and I looked back at them in kind.

"I'll carry him," said Joel.

He passed me the chickens and loaded me onto his back. The martens watched us in amazement. I was ashamed to be up there, incapable of keeping pace, but I noticed the frightened look on their faces. Maybe a big dog bending down to carry you wasn't something they saw every day. Maybe they thought that I was his master, crippled but formidable. I got over my shame in a hurry now that I was taller than them.

The Sunken Rock was a boulder sunk in the middle of a small pond. No sooner had we arrived, not knowing where we were going, than I began to look around feverishly for Anja and her eyes. If I heard a noise I would immediately turn my head, hoping to see her coming—a wonder to behold—to lead us to her den. I imagined talking with her, moving close to her, breathing in her scent. Then it came to me that there wouldn't be time. Joel wouldn't permit any delay. We would take the sacks and head home as soon as possible. This thought distressed me so much I decided I had to do something. I loosened the string around one of the chickens, tugging at it with my teeth when no one was looking.

The two martens led us to the foot of a tall tree, where I saw the entrance to their den; we stopped a short distance away on the bare ground that surrounded the roots. A little farther on I noticed a small coop under construction, where the first chicken we'd let them have was busy scratching.

The biggest marten I'd ever seen emerged from the den—an old creature with drowsy, watchful eyes. This was Sasha the Great.

"Hector, who are these creatures?" he said, pointing at us. "And why do they go around with one of them mounted on the other?" He stared at us, dumbfounded.

"They're the fox's servants, Papa. They've brought the hens."

Sasha nodded, not taking his eyes off us. "I imagine they'll be wanting their carrots," he said. "Silas!"

Moments later another male, more or less the same age as Hector but bald all over, came out of the den. Sasha told him to fetch the sacks and get some help. Hector went in after him, followed by Biko, who was, however, stopped in his tracks by the big marten's growl.

"Watch it, punk," he said.

Biko gulped and inched back toward us.

Out of the den came Hector, Silas, a pregnant female, and Anja, each carrying a sack of carrots. All of them, including her, looked at me and Joel with surprise. My heart beat harder, and I stood frozen to the spot, pinning back my ears.

"Today we can only take three," said Joel.

He let me down, bending low.

"As you wish," Sasha replied.

Anja watched as I walked up to Hector with the chickens in my paw. She too looked drowsy, but more beautiful than ever, standing there next to the others, as if she'd been designed by God himself.

I passed the chickens into her brother's hands, and my ploy paid off. No sooner had I loosened my grip on their legs than one of the chickens jerked free and fell to the ground; a moment later the other fluttered away as well, running in different directions. Hector went off like a shot on the trail of the first one, Joel chased the second, and Biko the third, stirring up a huge cloud of dust. The chickens hightailed it into the woods with the others on their trail. I found myself alone with Sasha and his family.

"Did you tie the knot around the chickens, cripple?" he said.

"Yes, sir."

He turned his back to me and headed toward the den. "You did a hell of a job," he said.

I saw that the females were going back in too. Silas, however, remained where he was.

"Wait!" I shouted.

The big marten stopped, and so did the others. Anja spun toward me. My excitement and boldness made me shiver.

"Your daughter," I said. "I want her."

Sasha the Great stood there incredulous for a few seconds, then burst out laughing. "You want my daughter, cripple? Which one?"

"Anja."

The big marten guffawed. "Then get in line, but I don't think you'll make it till fall."

Anja lowered her gaze and went into the den with her sister. Sasha the Great grunted and followed them. I stood there stunned, not knowing what to say.

Silas, seeing the state I was in, decided to relieve me of my embarrassment.

He told me that Sasha had been left alone with four children. The second child, Tess, had died two summers ago; she had been fought over by countless suitors, who, in the end, killed her. The same thing was happening with Anja. The season of mating had brought Fedor, followed by a male named Derry. Derry had killed Fedor in the forest, then started stealing carrots from man and offering them as gifts.

After that Biko turned up, put Derry to flight, and suggested buying some chickens and building a coop. Sasha had sat through this story before and decided to keep his daughter safe until fall. Whoever wanted her had to be able to wait and eliminate his rivals; he had to ask for her after the seasonal instinct had subsided. Hector was helping their father to enact this plan, and had remained alone for her sake. Silas, for his part, was the mate of the third-born, Dana, who was now expecting. They would go and live elsewhere once the kits were born, when the furor of summer had passed. He was sure that Derry would be turning up again, as would others. Biko was bigger and smarter than most, but he would still have to fight. Anyway, they were all typical bandits, infatuated with the most beautiful female they'd laid eyes on.

I listened to what he told me with great attention. In the meantime the others had returned with the chickens.

"Let it go, if you want to save your hide," said Silas.

Only then did I notice that Biko was standing there watching us. He had grasped some part of the exchange and was giving me a nasty look. Joel passed me a sack of carrots. The sun was already high in the sky.

"Let's get a move on," he said.

I'd never heard of such behavior. No male had ever done so much for his offspring. The fear of losing another daughter had made him crazy, but incredibly shrewd.

If you wanted one of his girls you had to prove it in earnest, even to yourself. It was an idea so just and proper, I thought, that it had almost nothing to do with the world we lived in.

We got back to Solomon's in the evening. Carrying the sack of carrots had taken a good deal out of me, though we met with no problems along the way. The old fox had fallen asleep in the kitchen chair. On the table there was a thing that made a noise, a polished river stone, with some carvings I recognized. It was an object of man's. I had never seen it previously; perhaps it had been given to him that very day, as payment. It emitted a continuous and reassuring noise, ticking and ticking. I noticed that some of the carvings were in reality sticks, and that these sticks were moving, spinning in a circle.

"Put that stuff down," wheezed the old fox, who had just come to.

"What's that thing?"

"Bad news."

"In what sense?"

"It counts how close you are to croaking. It's horrible."

I stared at the object, enthralled. It set my teeth on edge, yet it had given rise to a new perception inside me: what I was thinking at that moment struck me, precisely on account of its ticking, as precious.

"It's man's?" I asked.

"It belongs to someone who has no fear," he said. "Now do me a favor. Go to the brook and throw it in so I don't have to hear it anymore." He coughed loudly. "Then come back here so we can write."

I did not throw it in the brook. Instinct urged me to do so, but I restrained myself. There was something it was measuring that was closer at hand than my death. It was the arrival of autumn. It was Anja.

The next day we returned to Sasha the Great's den to retrieve the last three sacks. Although I'd been up writing for most of the night, I didn't feel tired at all. In spite of Solomon's fantastical dictations, reading his adventures excited me, and waiting to see Anja again, I was imagining some of my own.

We arrived in the late afternoon. No one was under the big tree. They were all still asleep. Silas emerged from a bush with a mouse in his mouth and startled when he saw us. Joel told him we had come for the carrots.

"They're hidden back here, come with me," he told us.

The dog followed him, but I remained rooted to the spot. The entrance to the den was dark. I couldn't see anyone. Without asking myself too many questions I picked up a stone and threw it inside, then hid behind a root. As quick as a flash, Hector appeared, on the alert, with his ears pinned back. By that time Joel had come back with Silas, and he spotted them. They exchanged a few words, and then, behind her brother, I saw Anja's muzzle poking out. She saw Joel and immediately began looking around for someone else. I shivered from head to tail.

I emerged from my hiding place, and sure enough she noticed me before the others. I took Solomon's polished stone, which I'd brought along, and presented it to her. I placed it on a root, then went off to join Joel, who passed me a sack of carrots. We left without a word of farewell, in complete silence. I looked back over my shoulder four times.

"Sasha the Great Big Idiot," the old fox had said. "Four chickens that don't lay eggs for ten sacks filled with carrots." He laughed, then started to cough. "God has made them all stupid. Thanks be to God," he wheezed.

That day we passed off carrots on everyone, at a high price, and I planted a few alongside the scraps of the ones we'd eaten. I remember that all I did was think about how to get Anja, how to chase away Biko, Derry, and whoever else. I felt strong, but not strong enough to go claw to claw with a real bandit, and besides, I was a cripple. One part of me knew that I had to let it go, but the other held fast to hope, got me daydreaming and carried away like the worst of temptations. I thought about Louise again and could clearly see a certain similarity with what I was experiencing now. I asked myself why I should go on the way I was, why I should give God the opportunity to hurt me again. But I went on just the same.

*

Two days later, in the middle of the night, I woke with a start. There was something at my window. I approached with caution, by the light of a lamp. Joel's big head was staring in at me.

"They're looking for you," he said.

I goggled my eyes. "Who?"

"You'd better come out."

I sneaked out through the window, not making a sound. The dog stood waiting a short distance away. He walked with me down to the bottom of the hill.

"Who's looking for me, Joel?" I asked again. I was beginning to worry.

The dog stopped in his tracks. "He is."

He pointed to a spot between the trees, where I made out the head of a marten in the dark.

"What does he want?" I asked, but the dog was already trotting back up the hill. Fear was forsaking me, little by little. If Joel had left me alone, that meant I wasn't in any danger. A tingle of excitement ran down my tail, and I went to meet my visitor.

Hector regarded me sternly. As I stepped nearer to him he did not greet me but merely told me to follow him. We walked a short way through the trees before he stopped. He'd brought me to a tiny space among three birches. There, waiting for me, was Anja. I held my breath and stood completely still, as if face-to-face with a ferocious animal. Hector left us alone.

She drew closer to me, an inch from my nose. Her scent was faint, sharp, and clean, like freshly cut grass. My legs went limp and my head spun for a moment. Her gaze transfixed me and slipped under my skin. It was impossible to hide anything from her.

"What is it?" she said. She held out the polished stone for me to see. Its ticking filled my ears, along with her voice, which was warm and thin, sweet and wavering. I stared at the stone, recovering some sense of reality.

"It belongs to man," I said. "It measures the before and the after."

Her eyes returned to me and I understood that the stone had nothing to do with this visit.

"The before and the after?" she asked.

"Man calls it *time*."

I restrained myself; I had no desire to reveal its real function.

"The arrival of autumn," I said.

She smiled, and her eyes smiled with her. "What's your name?"

"Archy."

She sighed and stepped even nearer. My heart urged me forward, but my paws wouldn't budge. She thrust her muzzle into my neck, then gently pushed and slipped herself between my paws. At that point instinct took over and I pulled her to me. She had a moment's hesitation, I saw her pupils wobble, then with a long sigh she pressed her belly to mine and let herself be taken. Our instincts were perfectly matched, they danced the same dance; time receded, and the world hid away. I lost myself in her, and she did the same. When the quiet came, while we were still clinging to each other, she gave me a frightened look.

"The arrival of autumn. I beg you," she said.

She stood up and ran off. I stood up too, but I saw her, already a long way off, running with her brother. A noise brought me back to myself.

It was the ticking of the stone, close at hand. She had left it for me.

*

Solomon had woken up and had come to fetch me to write, only to find me gone. I saw him hunched over the kitchen table intently reading a crumpled page with a gloomy look on his face. He must have dug through my things, looking for a clue to where I'd gone. I recognized the piece of paper immediately. It was the last page of my writing, the page on which I'd written about Louise. He lifted his gaze to me in shock and fury.

"I had the heart to teach you the truth about the world, and this is what you do with it?" he hissed.

"Solomon—"

He threw a plate at me, and it shattered against my muzzle. I could smell the burning meat. He was on his hind legs now.

"'God is cruel and mean'?" he quoted. "'He has cursed me and I detest him'?"

He sent another plate flying through the air, but I dodged it.

"Little bastard ass hair!" he thundered. "You don't deserve even to call him by his name, you shitty animal."

His fur bristling, he tore the sheet to shreds.

"If God wanted that sister of yours dead, it's because no one gave a damn about her! You can wipe your ass with your loves, you idiot!"

He flipped the table with a deafening crash, but this time Joel didn't come down.

"Do you want to know who is really cursed?" he went on. "I am cursed! For having allowed you to defile his name with all that shit you have in your head!"

He was overwhelmed by a coughing fit. I watched him bent

double by convulsions, trying to catch his breath, staggering toward his chair. Only then did he manage to get ahold of himself. The old fox looked at his paw, covered in blood; a trickle ran down from his mouth like a thread. His eyes went wide.

"Good God," he said, then fell to the ground.

12

Like an Animal

EVEN TODAY I find the sequence of events curious. How I went from great joy to tragedy in only seconds. Back then I thought it was God's malice, God meddling with my happiness, but now I can say that it was my existence that was out of place, the only anomaly in a design that was already staring me in the face.

I sent Joel to find a doctor, as fast as his feet would carry him. I dragged the old fox to his room, still unconscious; he was breathing heavily, his tongue lolling from his bloodstained mouth. An overpowering anxiety took possession of every part of me, replacing me bodily. In a sense it was if I'd disappeared from the room, leaving behind a trembling shadow, a mere noise beside the bed. I did nothing but sit there, not thinking about anything, my head hanging on by a spider's thread. The candlelight illuminated Solomon's frowning muzzle but sometimes flickered out entirely, making his face monstrous, and I closed my eyes, trying to remember it. I waited an interminable while. Then the dog returned with the doctor, the same one he had fetched for me. The doctor seemed even more frightened than the last time, what with his panting and his ruffled coat, his breath that still reeked of sleep. I told him what had happened, and while I talked he nodded, casting glances at the old fox, my tone only adding to his nervousness. Then he sat down on the bed and began his examination. An intolerable silence descended. He opened Solomon's mouth, peered at his tongue, listened to his breathing. Joel and I looked on expectantly. His treasures, the objects of man that he'd collected over a lifetime, were scattered around the room. He would never have allowed us to linger there; it would have made him furious. The thought must have occurred to both of us, because the dog went out a few moments later and sat waiting outside the door. When the beaver had finished his examination, he stood and looked at me. I didn't like his look at all. It left me even more anxious, my guts all knotted up. We went out of the room, and he fixed his gaze on both of us.

"I don't know what he's got," he said in a faint voice. He hunched, as if to defend himself from an attack, and took a breath. "But he's dying."

All three of us stood there completely still. The doctor's eyes leapt back and forth between us, trying to figure out what we intended to do. A long time passed. The feeling that I'd disappeared grew stronger, fear turned into certainty, and, in a sense, I became calm. Joel was the first to move, making his way slowly to the window only to stop again. That horrible silence was too much for the doctor.

"I don't know what he's got," he repeated, but neither of us offered a word or gesture in response.

The sun was rising behind the trees, coloring the sky blue. That's when I heard the old fox cough, wheezing weakly. I rushed into his room and saw that he had opened his eyes and was gazing straight at me.

"I'm thirsty," he said.

He was not lucid, he was trying to lick his own nose, while his head still lay flat against the bed. When I brought him some water, he seemed to perk up a little. He noticed my face.

"What happened?" he rasped.

I took a deep breath. "You're sick, Solomon."

He didn't take his eyes off me. He understood at once.

"Go get the pen," he said.

"So be it. God is calling me home to him."

The old fox gave a glimmer of a smile. He could no longer bring himself to dictate, so I had to write by myself, recasting the sentences aloud. He would nod at me if he found them good. I saw that he was serene, and this gave me the strength to concentrate, no matter how small and useless I felt.

"He will take me to Heaven, with his children, like a man."

Before he spoke he drew deep breaths, and I paused to listen. I think he was talking more to himself than to me. It was a way of maintaining his fortitude.

"God is with me, God is on my side."

"Of course," I replied. Then I went back to writing. We hadn't allowed the doctor to leave, but then he hadn't asked to. Perhaps out of fear, he remained sitting by the entrance. Suddenly he scuttled off to the kitchen to fix a painkiller for the fox.

"Someday you'll die too," Solomon told him, bitterly.

I saw the doctor shudder, but I knew he didn't fully grasp the meaning of those words. Meanwhile, Joel had scarcely moved from the window, and he hadn't touched his food; he stared off into the distance, apparently at nothing.

"Don't hate him," the old fox said at one point.

"Hate who?"

"You wrote that you hate God, because your sister is dead."

I attempted a smile. "That was nonsense, Solomon."

He was overcome by a spasm of coughing. He turned his head toward the window.

"I loved too, believe me. All my affection brought me was disgrace and confusion. Even the most luminous love of all—"

He broke off. I could see him lost in ferocious recollection.

"When we love someone, we always feel the opposite for someone else. God is the only one who can be loved in holy peace."

I nodded. I picked up the pen again.

The den had descended into a total silence more overwhelming than the noise of the forest. Any clients who ventured up the hill Joel drove away, and soon no one dared to come out of the trees. Whenever Solomon fell asleep, I went to the kitchen. I felt more dead than alive, in a state of suspension; inside that room, the only body breathing was the body of the old fox, enormous and serene, waiting on the bed. The thought of Anja was my only relief.

The doctor came into the kitchen. I only noticed his presence when I heard dishes rattling. He ate but as if he were not in his body, serving himself without savor.

"Do you have a family?" it occurred to me to say.

He started, as if surprised to have to talk to me.

"Two children and a mate. We live down by the dams."

I knew the place. I'd been through there once with Joel. A wide stream drained by the beavers.

"They'll be worried."

"Oh, yes—and how. You abducted me in the middle of the night."
He lowered his gaze, as though to beg my pardon. "This is the finest
den I've ever been in," he said.

He passed me a plate with two eggs and some herbs.

"What's your name?" I asked.

"Tuck."

I began to eat. He watched in silence, not sitting down. He had
something to say, but he kept chewing the cud without spitting
it out.

"Go home if you want," I said, beating him to it.

The beaver started again. Nervously, he massaged the fur on his
head.

"Oh, no, I . . ." he stammered. "In fact I'd like to stay a little longer,
I want to be of help."

As he said this he looked quite sincere, full of compassion. I sat
there without knowing what to say, since pity is very rare in an
animal. I looked at him in perplexity, then let my gaze fall on the
plate in his paw—a capacious plate, meant for Joel. The silence of
the den resounded in my ears, and I wondered what I looked like,
whether I looked alive or dead.

"Do what you want," I said.

The beaver nodded and left the kitchen, went back to being
a shadow wandering around the den. It was clear to me that to be a
doctor you have to feel a peculiar need to take care of others. It is a
feeling I have never experienced, and it seemed to me a stupid thing.

"You have to bury me. Dig a big hole, then put me inside."

Solomon had put an end to my writing, telling me he didn't want to go on with it anymore. He asked me to reread passages in the word of God about Heaven and souls being saved.

"That's how men do it, they bury each other," he murmured. "Their bodies go into the earth and their souls into the sky. I don't want to be torn to pieces by the first creature who comes along."

I nodded at everything he said, even when he contradicted himself.

"I leave you all my treasures, bury them with me."

Some of his spasms made him writhe, and he clutched his paws to his chest, from which his breath came strangled. He spit blood and then licked his nose, dirtying his muzzle. I gave him water but he did not drink; we had already stopped trying to get him to eat.

"Read to me again, again."

When he heard verses about salvation he sighed deeply, closing his eyes, apparently asleep. At the end of certain sentences he nodded, forcing a smile, making me feel petty—in the grip of a fear that had no effect on him at all.

I was an animal and, after my death, nothing else awaited me.

Joel didn't touch his food and spent his time staring into the void or pacing aimlessly around the hill. He looked bewildered, hostile at times, but as bland as ever, as though there were no one home inside his skull.

I told him that a hole had to be dug, and he asked me where before resuming his aimless pacing. Where exactly the hole ought to go I hadn't considered, and Solomon hadn't given any instructions. I jumped up on the boulder above the den; Joel was circling the hill, along the line of trees, stopping from time to time to look around him; over at the coop, I could see the worried doctor feeding the chickens. The sun scorched the tall grass, which stood motionless in the absence of breeze. I saw the apple tree, casting its shadow all around, laden with unripe apples. I remembered when I was tethered to that tree and ordered by the old fox to gather up all the apples, and how, because of one apple, man was cursed by God. I decided that was where the hole ought to go. It took me a long time to catch Joel's attention. He seemed to not hear my voice, and he went on ignoring me until I was smack-dab in front of his nose. I pointed out the spot to him, and he started digging and digging, until the sun went down. I tried to help him but he pushed me away and growled, so that I was left standing there watching him. The doctor brought us something to eat, but Joel didn't touch it; he kept going in spite of his empty stomach. When I told him it was deep enough, he cleaned the dirt from his nose and went back to his rounds. The hole he had made was cavernous, and the shadow of the apple tree lay at rest there. The beaver took his plate and headed back to the den, and for a while I watched Joel wandering, lost, without any meaning or direction, around the hill. He was protecting the old fox against death, which he may well have expected to emerge out of the trees like a stranger or an unwanted client.

That night Solomon wanted to go on with his writing, but we made it only a few pages. His attention wandered, and he was unable to touch up the sentences I was reinventing in place of his. I could tell his mood was darkening.

"That's fine," he wheezed, forcing a smile. "I leave it to you."

He gave me his paw. I held it and looked into his eyes. These eyes that had once scorched me with their life were now powerless, bloodshot circles. But I saw a glint there, a flicker of lucidity that struck fear in me and compelled me still. I nodded.

"Finish it for me. It wants love," he said.

"Of course, Solomon."

"And burn the old one. So that no one knows who I was."

I hesitated. He sensed it and squeezed my paw tighter. His book told the story of an extraordinary life full of malicious deeds, blood, ruses, and deceptions. My heart broke at the thought of that drive and determination—letting go of it would be like letting go of a piece of the world. His story meant everything to me. It had colored my dreams more than the word of God. It spoke of us.

"Do it," the old fox said with a sigh. "Just tell the tale of an animal, and his stupid intentions."

I told him I would. Solomon let go of my paw. He stared out the window.

"How long this night is. It seems he wants to keep us with him forever, miserable and clueless."

I couldn't understand what he was saying. He produced mangled words, meaningless phrases meant for no one, which he pronounced like solemn truths. A violent spasm shook him. I saw his eyes go wide, and his sudden panic.

"Bring me the box," he commanded.

I placed it next to him, opening it as I had seen him do. The little figure danced out, and the old harmonious noise resounded in the room. Solomon closed his eyes for a few moments, but I could see he was holding his breath. He made a horrible grimace, and all at once that noise became intolerable, drilling into his ears.

He opened his eyes, breathing faster and grinding his teeth.

"I'm afraid," he said.

He looked around him in every direction, grabbed my fur with one paw and pulled me toward him.

"I'm afraid," he shouted, beginning to weep.

Instinctively I recoiled and he looked at me in desperation, as if I were forsaking him. I tried to get ahold of myself, only to recoil again and more. I didn't know what to do, I was terrified. I picked up the word of God and attempted to read a passage about Heaven, but the fox started to scream and hurled the box aside, knocking the book from my paws.

"No! No!"

Tears ran down his muzzle. Once again, he began spitting blood; he tried to grab me and I let him; he pulled me close to him. I started to weep too. I felt his fear, and I saw the pain in his eyes. There was no longer any salvation left in that room.

"What should I do? What should I do?" I asked in a strangled voice, my nose clogged with snot.

"I don't want to die, I beg you, I don't want to die!"

He wept harder, and I wept harder with him, because neither of us could do a thing about it. We were together, but he was alone.

He coughed loudly, spewing blood, thrusting his muzzle into my chest as if to hide.

"I beg you, please, I beg you."

I wasn't saying anything anymore, I was just crying and trembling.

"I beg you, please."

He was not asking God, he was speaking to me. God's name I never heard him say again.

"I don't want to, that's all, I don't want to!"

He took his muzzle from my chest. I was drenched with the tears from his fiery eyes, full of terror and desperation that overwhelmed my own. His gaze had more life than a newborn cub, his darting pupils lighting up his tears and clinging to anything just to be alive one more moment, no matter how worthless or insignificant. Like a tempest, resistless, he gathered me up and laid hold of all my secrets, every feeling I'd ever had; he grabbed me and took me where he was going, whether Heaven or nowhere at all.

Then his pupils emptied, his grip on my fur loosened, and his breathing slowed.

"I beg you," he said, and those were his last words; he fell back weightless on the bed, and the tears ceased. His gut shuddered, sank, and was still.

These were the last moments of Solomon the lender.

In the end, saved or not, he hadn't gone away with a smile, he hadn't pleaded with God; like an animal, he had begged whoever was by the side of his bed, still hoping he'd rise again. Perhaps that's the lesson death has to teach those who know it will come—that it's a journey you make alone, through the self's meanders, where everything vanishes even as you try to retrieve it.

His gaze had turned toward the ceiling. In his eyes, deep beneath the fear, I could see a beautiful calm. He had gone with God, of that I'm sure; God was waiting for him on the other side. I sat down in the chair and wiped away my tears, remaining there in silence for a long time. By now the candle at his side had burned down. Darkness descended on his body, and with it the longest of nights. I picked up the word of God and put it away, along with the box, which no longer made noise even when it was open. A strangled scream made me jump. I rushed out of the den and saw Joel, close by, letting someone have it. When I drew nearer he looked as if he wanted to attack me too, but he restrained himself once he recognized me. Beneath him lay the body of the beaver, his throat severed. In his paw he held a clump of herbs, which he'd probably run to get when he'd heard the fox scream. The dog had mistaken him for an intruder.

He was still moving—and still had the strength to look in my direction. With a gurgle, widening his eyes, he let the herbs fall from his paw and brought it to his throat.

"They're no use now," I told him.

I turned to Joel and his bloody muzzle.

"He's dead."

The dog didn't respond, he simply took to pacing around the hill again, leaving us by ourselves. With another gurgle, the beaver let his paw fall to the ground, and in a short while he was gone too.

I couldn't bring myself to attend to him. I went back into the den and climbed into my bed. I didn't sleep, but I didn't have any thoughts either. I waited for the daylight to arrive.

At dawn I laid the fox's body in the hole. It was so light it felt hollow, and I didn't even have to strain my paw. Joel had quit pacing. Now he was sitting at the edge of the trees with his back to me, staring straight ahead. The birds were singing very loudly.

I chose a few treasures to bury with Solomon because there wasn't space for all of them. He was lying at the bottom of the hole, looking up at the sky, and I placed them around him the way they'd been in his room.

I went back into the kitchen and transcribed the last part of his book without stopping, changing what he would have wanted to change, putting in words about God. I didn't eat, and I didn't touch water. I read every page that he had filled, until they turned blank. His last words described the work of a lender and the hill. He knew that he was old, that his adventures were over, and that he would die there. Knowing he would die in that particular place was what tormented him most; it was always near, in his dreams and his thoughts; it waited for him in every room, behind every door, narrowing the gap between him and the horizon. He wrote about his life as a man and he wrote about Heaven, cursed his horrible destiny, and asked for another soon to come. At a certain point I started to think I was dying too. Perhaps it was exhaustion. I felt my heart leap in my chest and a throbbing behind the eyes. I let go of the pen and leaned over the table, bent double. A sort of terror crept in between my ears, and I prepared myself for what I had witnessed the previous night. By the time I had this thought, however, the sickly sensation had already passed. The only thing left was the certainty that my last moments would be the same as his. I would scream, I would cry, and I would pray to whoever there was to pray to, even God. Strangely I didn't despair, but then these thoughts were without true meaning to me in that moment. I went back to writing.

I finished when dusk was falling, picked up the new book, and went outside. Joel hadn't budged. A crow had plucked out one of the fox's eyes and flew off with it as soon as he saw me. Had he known whose eye it was—that it belonged to the shrewdest bandit ever seen in these parts—perhaps he wouldn't have eaten it. Solomon's body lay there one-eyed, staring at the sky. I placed his book between his paws.

I called Joel three times before he turned his head. I shouted that the earth had to be moved. The big black dog came to me, but when he saw the fox he stopped, as if turned to stone. I began to bury him, and after a little while the dog joined in. Solomon's face disappeared beneath the soil. It was the last time I would see him. I believe Joel was thinking the same thought. Solomon had taught me to read, to write, and to labor. He had opened my eyes to the world and our painful, ephemeral existence. He had taught me to worship a God who would not save us, but who would save him from his greatest terror. Disappearing. As he was doing now. As would we all. Wordlessly I said farewell to my master for the last time, and the earth reclaimed him, along with his things, his new book in one paw and the word of God in the other.

13

The Missing Words

IN THE DAYS THAT FOLLOWED I went on doing my usual chores.
I fetched water for the big basin in the kitchen, fed the chickens, cut
the overgrown grass. I left the doctor's body among the trees. He had
been killed for his compassion. I felt sorry for his two children and
his mate, who would be left alone; but then again it had been his
choice, his express wish, to stay, and therefore there wasn't much to
be said. Joel didn't budge from under the apple tree. He lay exhausted
by the fox's grave, staring into the void. It became clear to me that
he meant to die so I tried to make him eat, but he was still strong,
and I was taking my life in my paws. The hill had sunk into a gloomy
torpor, as if the sun no longer beat down on it as before. A rabbit
came climbing up to the den to do a deal, but I told him all dealing
was done now that the old fox was dead. The clientele dwindled.

I had no interest in possessing more than I needed and felt no
pleasure in the abundance of food or in the things of man. I liked
these treasures because Solomon had liked them. I was beginning
to realize how thoroughly I was bound to that fox, and how fond
I'd become of him. A profound sense of futility sapped my strength.
With his old book open in front of me, I sat in the kitchen through
the night, staring at his empty chair, weeping, and cursing God.

When I climbed into bed, I heard a steady sound I'd heard before. It was the little whisper of the instrument of man. Lately I'd been ignoring it, abandoning myself to a bitter sleep. Now its ticking called to me. Anja rose up from my torpid thoughts, wriggled loose from the grip of my sadness, and shone like a star. I saw her waiting for me at the Sunken Rock, all beautiful, in the first days of fall. I thought about our encounter in the trees, about how she'd looked at me before we twined together, and how I'd promised that I would come back for her.

I opened my eyes and stood up. The desire to keep moving brought me back to life. I wondered how long it would be until fall came. I wondered whether Biko had been succeeded by another suitor, whether Derry had returned, or some other strong, iron-willed male. I was going to have to fight, to risk my hide, but I wasn't afraid. Darkness drained from the room, and the sun peeked over the horizon. My heart beat harder.

I finished harvesting the grapes, took some eggs from the coop, and prepared a solid meal for Joel. The dog was still lying beside the grave. He did not notice me until I was very close.

"Eat or you'll die," I said to him.

He didn't respond and gave no sign of having heard me. I left the plate and went back inside. From the kitchen window, I could see the sun was beating down on him mercilessly. He was a splotch of color splayed on the ground. He needed a reason to live other than Solomon, something to give him the strength to go on.

That night I mixed water and grape juice in a bowl and went out. I tiptoed up behind him. He was asleep. Darting toward him,

I grabbed his head, pulled it toward me, and poured the contents of the bowl into his mouth. He coughed, but he had swallowed some of it, and before he could turn and bite me I was already safely away. Joel stood up and saw who it was, but he didn't come after me. He coughed a few times, then sat down. I went back into the kitchen and spied on him through the window. He didn't vomit, which pleased me. It meant I'd bought a little time.

I didn't try anything like that again. He was on the alert now and kept his ears pricked. I continued to give him food, setting it down as soon as I got close enough for him to growl. It was always still full when I retrieved it. In the meantime I worked with great zeal. I forced myself to do more than I had to do; I carried the water to the kitchen taking a longer route and started gathering firewood for winter early. I thought that by toiling away like that I would strengthen my body and make it possible to fight for Anja. Joel's gaze followed my doings, and I imagined he wondered what I was up to and if I wasn't perhaps hatching some new plan. His nose had cracked in the heat, and flies landed on the sores. He shook his head when they bit him, but he didn't exactly bother to chase them off.

I read the fox's book while on the kitchen table the little whisper ticked blithely on. I read about how agile he'd been as a youngster, not all that strong but capable of defending himself. He'd fought with larger animals, not suffering any wounds, and survived by killing them with trickery or guile. When he was at a disadvantage inspiration seemed to whisper in his ear until he found a way forward. I clutched the little whisper in my paw, and I waited for a sign. For a brief moment, I saw the old fox in his chair by the fireplace, wrapped in his blanket. He looked at me, trying to discern what was in my head.

"Love is for the stupid," he said.

I heaved a long sigh, put down the little whisper, and closed the book. But just before I closed it, I happened to pause on the first page. At the bottom, off to the side, were the first words the fox had ever written, badly copied from the word of God, imbued with his blood. I had read those words more times than I could count, and still they shook me.

"God said 'Let there be light!' And there was light."

"Aren't you afraid of dying, Joel?" I shouted.

I was climbing the hill with four buckets of water, watching him. He lay motionless in his usual spot. Halfway up, I felt a twinge in my paw and fell. I'd been overdoing it. I stood up and contemplated the toppled buckets. As soon as I tried to pick them up, I fell again. Panting all the time, the big black dog lay there with his eyes tight shut. I was panting too: the pain had knocked the wind out of me.

He was still beautiful. His gaze went past the flies and past me, up to the sky and the trees. He wasn't afraid and, lying there in the grass on the side of the hill, I envied him. I felt very alone.

My paw now hurt so much I could use it only to feed the chickens. For a cripple to triumph over a healthy male was almost impossible: the thought tormented me. The shadows in the kitchen became bristling martens and Biko's face stared back out of the water in the basin. The little whisper robbed me of sleep, and I began to think that, instead of measuring the time until autumn, it was making a mockery of Joel's life. He was slipping away, and I couldn't pull him back however much I wanted to. He couldn't just choose to die. What a dirty trick! It wasn't for him or for God to play it on me.

Idleness made me restless. The den still spoke of Solomon: to me it seemed he'd just gone out to watch the sunset. The board with the list of clients was in its place, with the pen beside it, above the sacks of provisions; his blanket still lay in a corner near the entrance. The scents were the same, and in each room I was driven—as in snatches of dream—to see the things I'd seen before repeat and repeat. My stomach churned, and my nose twitched, struck by an invisible paw. I felt suffocated, and I decided that I needed to make the den mine. But at the door to Solomon's room, I froze, momentarily terrified of being caught going through his things. "Get out of here, ass hair!" I seemed to hear.

It was not easy for me to handle his treasures. They were disinclined toward my paws, ready to break or fling themselves to the ground, not recognizing their master. Or perhaps I felt unworthy of them, worried about being clumsy with these things fashioned for the hands of man. I thought of throwing them away, but I couldn't bring myself to do it. I stacked them in a corner of the room, half out of sight; the gloomy objects and framed figures observed me, but I wasn't the one they were waiting for. I decided to unmake the bed. It wasn't his anymore, yet his blood was still there. Under the straw mattress where he'd laid his head there were some bundles of paper. They were scraps, and I realized as I leafed through them that I'd found the missing pieces of his old book. I sat down on the bed and started to read. There were things written there that he'd never told me. I felt I didn't know him, and my head reeled. No doubt these were stories he'd wanted to forget, stories he'd hidden from himself and God. Secrets. Solomon had set fire to a forest. He had killed his only love.

He also wrote that he had left his gang of bandits when he found

138

God. He had discovered a treasure, he said, something greater than food, but a creature named Gilles, one of his companions, had tried to steal it from him, turning the others against him.

For two weeks he wandered, until he met a dog who lived with a human family. Her name was Ljuba, and she had a pup. Since the children in the family were learning to read and write, she'd picked up some of it too, but she didn't confide in the fox. She didn't trust him. So Solomon abducted the pup in the dead of night and forced the dog to teach him what he needed to know to understand what his treasure contained. For two months he'd hidden the puppy away, meeting Ljuba elsewhere and ignoring her yelps, her constant pleas to have her young one back. He forced her to follow the children's lessons, to pay closer attention, and to transmit it all to him. At the conclusion of their tête-à-têtes he sucked the milk from her nipples and spat in a bowl to feed the little one. Never had he seen so much hatred in anyone's eyes, the fox wrote.

In the end, when he was able to read and write, he took the pup with him. The little one reminded him of his love, the dog who'd once been his companion. He named him Joel.

A shiver ran down my spine. I pinned back my ears and went on reading.

Solomon grew fond of Joel. He taught him how to make his way through the woods, how to fight, how to pick up scents. For a long time they shifted from place to place. Solomon was convinced that his old companions were after him. He'd run away with something that had belonged to them too. The pup grew and became the big black dog now languishing on the ground beside his abductor's grave, bound to him like flesh to bone. After all, that was Solomon's power. He may have dragged us into his life, but he'd made us what we were. We were his, and he was ours. I understood Joel's suffering, and stained the page I was reading with a tear.

Our lives would have been different without him, and perhaps better; but I still believe we were destined to meet, God willed it, the dog for one reason and I for another.

Among those pages I found one passage in which he talked about me. He said I reminded him of man because I had eyes that understood. He said I was his most precious treasure. I was like him.

For a long time I sat there in silence, smiling faintly. He hadn't written anything more after that. His book was truly finished.

I went out to see Joel. In one paw I held a plate with food and in the other the secret pages. He growled when I came close, but I didn't run away. I set the plate down.

"You don't come from a wasps' nest," I said.

The dog growled louder, baring his teeth.

"Solomon lied to you."

"What do you mean?"

At last, I was hearing his voice. I showed him the pages.

"These are words. They are bound to the paper, on which they remain. They reveal your true story, where you came from, who you are."

Joel stood up.

"You weren't born from a wasps' nest. You have a mother, and I know where she is."

"Tell me," he said.

I pointed to the plate. "Eat."

The dog studied me for a long while, trying to sniff out the trick. In his eyes I now detected a glimmer of curiosity, a foothold in the life that he'd been letting slip away. He came toward me, and right away I scuttled off. He put his paw to the plate, still staring at me.

"Are you telling the truth?" he asked.

"Yes. True as what is true to God."

He wavered. I was silent. He picked up the bowl and hurled it away as far as possible, almost falling over, before going to lie down again in his spot under the apple tree. I headed back inside.

While I was making dinner I heard the kitchen door slam shut. I saw him in the entryway, leaning against the jamb with his mouth hanging open. Shrunken as he was, the room was still too small for him. I ran to the far side of it and flattened myself against the wall. Joel swallowed with difficulty, then trudged to the table and sat down. His head collapsed onto his paws. He didn't have the energy to hold himself upright. Not a word was spoken.

"Do you want to eat?" I asked.

Wearily, with a gesture of his head, he said yes.

Though he had no desire to, he wolfed down what I gave him. I watched as the mouthfuls disappeared down his throat.

"Tell me the story," he murmured.

"You have to eat," I said softly, lowering my ears.

"I've eaten. Now tell me the story."

He was waiting for me to say something, his tired body holding up his giant head, torment in his eyes. I moved over to the window; if he tried to attack me, I'd be able to escape. Without moving, the dog tracked me.

"You have to eat more if you want to hear it."

The silence that followed made every muscle in my body taut. I was ready to jump. Joel stood and turned his back to me, staggering back to the apple tree and his master's grave.

The next day he came for lunch and dinner, as he did on the days after. He did not ask me his question again. He ate and then went back to the tree. I enjoyed his company, even if we sat in silence without a glance. He ate quickly, and when he rose from the table I was always on my toes. A story bound us, and the words to tell it were hidden beneath my tongue. No doubt he would have preferred to kill me than to sit together at the table. He was no longer the dog I had gone around the forest with. He was living for a promise. Mouthful by mouthful, he was waiting for me to set him free. And so the flesh began to return to his bones, and the little whisper went back to singing of the fall to come. I had won, God hadn't taken him, and I felt better for it. At night I dreamed of Anja. Summer was on the wane.

"Let's agree on something, Joel."

He was eating his dinner when I spoke. The dog looked me over. He was strong again. He quit chewing.

"I've eaten. Now tell me the story."

He slid the plate forward, still half full. I lowered my ears.

"Not yet."

Joel bared his teeth and arched his back. I swallowed down my food, pushing back my fear.

"I've eaten. Now tell me the story," he growled.

I cleared my throat. "First we need to come to an agreement," I said.

"Or I kill you?"

His whole body was pointed at me, ready to let loose. Very slowly I started to slip out of my chair.

"Kill me and you'll never know, the dead don't talk, and you're no reader," I said.

No response. He crept closer. My pounding heart threatened to split my chest.

"And Solomon wouldn't want it."

And Joel stopped in his tracks. His eyes went dead. They looked right through me, off into the distance. He shivered and shook himself. The fox's chair was in its usual spot by the fireplace. The dog looked at me. His teeth were still visible, but his face now was twisted with pain.

"What do you want?" he asked.

"A favor."

14

The Duel, the Farewell

When the first leaves began to fall, I set out for the Sunken Rock, in search of a female yet again. I thought of Louise. The image of my sister in the snow was as sharp as ever, and fraught with pain, a thorn lodged under my skin. This time, I told myself, things would end differently. Late in the afternoon, I arrived at Sasha the Great's den. The coop was built but there were no chickens; when they realized the hens didn't lay eggs they must have eaten them. I could see Hector standing in the shadow on the far side of the tree. His look was stern.

"You've come," he said.

"I promised."

"I didn't think you'd show."

It was clear he had no respect for me—the small, crippled stone marten who'd put himself in contention for his sister. Whatever male I had to take on would be a strong and healthy animal, practiced at killing. Hector dove into the opening to call his father. Moments later I was face-to-face with Sasha the Great in all his bulk. Anja was with him. Her face was lit up, as beautiful as could be. Then a shadow came over it.

"Have you come back here for my daughter, cripple?" the old marten said.

"Yes."

I saw her stiffen, frightened on my behalf. Sasha grunted.

"Then you'll have to wait for Biko. He's on the hunt."

So Biko was still the one. He had prevailed over the others. The strongest and most determined of all. For some reason, I thought about Mathias—about his face when I went back to my mother's den, as he sat in my seat, perfectly at ease, having gotten rid of my brothers. The thought passed quickly and filled me with rage. We waited for a while, until the sun was close to setting. I rested from my journey, and Sasha flashed me an ugly smile. He popped a few grapes in his mouth.

"Your hens didn't lay any eggs," he said.

"Don't I know it."

The big marten spit out a seed. "If you weren't about to die, I'd kill you myself."

I held my tongue. I watched Anja whisper to Hector.

The trees stood quite still, joining in our silence; every now and then a leaf fell from a branch, struggled in the air, and clattered on the ground. I was sitting on the bare spot by the protruding roots, breathing slowly. Sasha had taken a seat too. He stared at me with disgust, savoring my fear. His children sat close together beside him. The wordless peace of the whole scene gnawed at my soul, second by second, bit by bit. Birds sang softly.

Biko sprang out from the trees with a pheasant in his mouth, and no sooner did I see him than I was on my feet. He stopped in his tracks. He recognized me. His fur bristled and his breath came quick, his muscles still tense from running. As his chest heaved, the scars appeared and disappeared on his dark coat. His teeth gripped the powerless pheasant by its broken neck, its wings outspread. When my nose picked up the scent of him, I shuddered. It was musky and strong and overpowering, as if it too had to be defeated. I did not back down. The image of Leroy passed before my eyes, with the crow he'd caught, and then Mathias, with my mother's trinket. I was overcome by despair, the same despair I'd felt as I slept beside my brother, who seemed so mountainous. Then the rage returned and urged me on. Dumbstruck, Biko turned to Sasha.

"This dirty rotten crippled little liar intends to challenge you," he said. "Get it over with quickly."

Contemptuous as they were, these words filled me with pride. I was a suitor, and my challenge had to be met, even if I was the weaker and smaller one, and frightening to no one at all. But I saw myself now as a real animal, with teeth and claws.

Biko dropped the pheasant.

"Let's go somewhere else," I said.

"Oh, no! I want to see you croak right here, you little shit! I want to heft your head in my paws!" Sasha shouted.

At that, Biko shook himself.

"Get out of here," he hissed. "If you value your life."

I didn't move. I refused to tremble. I swallowed my fear back down.

"Let's go somewhere else," I repeated.

"Yes, get away from here," Anja broke forth, to everyone's surprise. "I don't want to see it."

Without saying a word, Sasha gave his daughter a sidelong glance. She was staring at Biko, her eyes begging him so intensely he was

146

forced to yield. The young male lowered his head, bowed slightly, and turned back to me.

"All right, let's go."

Sasha laughed. "Farewell," he said.

"Farewell," we replied, both of us certain his salutation didn't apply to us.

Biko led the way down to the Sunken Rock—to a spot right beside the pond. Gliding over the water, the dusky sunlight landed on the shore. A pair of birds heard us coming and took flight. Silence followed. The shadows of the trees had retreated, and in the clear light we could take the measure of the ground. Biko stood still. All the way there he'd kept his back to me, sure of himself, glancing back over his shoulder from time to time, more astonished than anxious. Keeping up with him was a struggle, my paw hurt, but not once along the way did I lose sight of him.

Now that we were face-to-face at the edge of the pond, his astonishment was double. He hadn't expected me to follow him all the way there, and he would never have imagined me as his ultimate opponent, going up against his enormous bulk as the sun went down and the leaves descended. We felt no hatred for each other, we just wanted the same thing, and to kill each other for it was the done thing. I saw a familiar expression come over his face. The fire in his eyes subsided, and our gazes met. He looked at me with pity.

"Get out of here and save your life," he said. "There will be other summers."

My blood boiled. He saw my eyes blaze, my paws stiffen, my chest swell. I pressed my ears flat against my head.

147

"The summer is over," I replied. "And there will be no need for others."

At that point he did as I had done: he lowered his ears, and he began to circle me. I didn't draw back or retreat at all; I bared my teeth, but I did not lunge. Biko edged closer, circling around, changing directions, trying to disorient me. I had no fear, and that perplexed him. When I stumbled, giving him an opening, he was on me in an instant. I heard him scream in pain as his jaws loosened from my neck. He had punctured my flesh, but he hadn't managed to sink his teeth in. I broke away in time to see the expression of surprise on his agonized face as, with a few brief spasms, he left this life. Having followed us down there, Joel had sprung from hiding and snapped his neck with one bite. With a groan, and without looking at either of us, Biko died. As the beating of my heart grew calm, I thought there must be no sweeter way to die.

Hector emerged from a bush. He'd seen what had happened. Joel turned on him with a growl, but I stopped him in his tracks.

Hector nodded at me, then slipped off between the branches. Pulling hard, the dog ripped Biko's head off his body.

"Sasha said he wanted one," he said.

I returned with the trophy and laid it at the big marten's feet. He looked at me with the sort of terror usually reserved for a wolf. Anja remained impassive.

"Liar, it must be a trick!" he thundered, but though he glared at me, he kept his distance.

"I saw it happen," said Hector, adding nothing more.

Biko's head was still bleeding, its mouth open and its tongue lolling out. Anja went right past it and hurled herself toward me, landing at my side.

"Come back here!" her father commanded, but she paid him no mind. Hector remained rooted to the spot.

"We're off," I said.

Sasha looked a long time at his daughter, sounding her soul. He could see that she'd made her choice. His face filled with contempt.

"Stupid. Take her then, I don't want to see her again. Between the two of you, you'll have a very short life."

And with those words he turned his back on us and went into his den. The sun had left a long red trail behind it, just like Biko's head. Hector came to say farewell to his sister.

"Thank you," she said, and he narrowed his eyes, bowed his head, and touched it to hers. When he turned to me, however, he wore a stern expression and looked me over from top to tail, as if to see if I really existed.

"I hope that dog of yours goes on protecting you forever," he said. I nodded.

Joel was waiting for us a short distance away and loaded us both onto his back. Anja looked at me as though I were the most beautiful hearth in the world.

"What happened to your face?"

She pointed to a place I couldn't see. Right next to my nose. There was a rough spot where no fur grew anymore. It was from the dish that Solomon had thrown at me before he'd gotten sick. I hadn't thought about him for several days.

"It's nothing," I replied. She nuzzled my chest. We threaded our way back through the night together. I had kept my promise, and I felt alive, again.

Anja stayed awake all night, as martens do. First thing, she asked about Solomon, and I told her he was dead without going into detail. I showed her around the den, then carried her up to the top of Joel's boulder and told her that, as far as the grass grew, everything was ours. She was very happy and smiled with her mouth and with her eyes. I don't think she had any idea what riches were. But I had gotten her and knew what it was to be rich. The fox had left me plenty: there was no need to hunt, no danger, no thirst or hunger. I had enough to feed my children and my grandchildren; I could have become the father of a big family, gone back to doing deals, and taught reading and writing. With this dream in my head, I lay down, begging my mate's pardon but I lived during the day and was spent. I fell asleep immediately, and it was the least troubled sleep I can recall.

The next morning Joel was waiting for me by the apple tree: the time had come to compensate him. Anja was still awake, and she watched as I took out Solomon's book.

"What's that?" she asked.

It occurred to me to hide it. But instead I held it out for her to see, unopened. I smiled at her. "These are words."

Somehow she realized it was better not to ask any more questions. As the day wore on, I discovered that Anja always knew what was going through my head. She didn't go with me to see Joel. She could tell it was something I wanted to do alone.

I walked out to him. The grass was already growing on Solomon's grave, and the ground was packed solid. The big black dog sat there, looking down expectantly. I opened the book and read him his story.

He listened in silence, not once lifting his head. When I finished the last sentence he appeared to be asleep, he was so consumed by his thoughts. With a jolt, which sent me flying, he shot me a watery-eyed glance. It was the first and last time I saw him weep. It must have been the first time for him too, because he kept making awful grimaces, squinching his eyes shut with every tear.

"Where is this place?" he murmured.

The fox hadn't written down the specifics. The last few days I'd been thinking about what to tell him, even before we set out for the Sunken Rock. I didn't want to deceive him, but it was the only thing I could think to do, to keep him from pining to death or killing me when he found out I didn't have a clue.

"Solomon told me about a den at the foot of a wooded hill," I said. "He told me it was beyond the mountain, where three rivers part ways."

I pointed to the farthest mountains. The dog looked. He was still weeping.

"That's all he wrote. I'm sorry."

Joel lost control of himself completely, sobbed, and let his head slowly fall until his brow touched the ground where we'd buried the fox. He pressed down hard, furrowing the earth, covering himself with dirt. He cried all the tears he had in one go. Then he stood, looked up at the mountains, and set off without a word of farewell.

Anja came to join me as he disappeared into the trees.

"Is he going away?" she said.

"Yes."

"Was it the words?"

"It was."

I never saw him again.

He went off searching for a place that didn't exist, beyond the wrong mountains, where no three rivers parted ways. He would wander all his life, clinging to a spurious hope, the only thing that made him keep going, like a phantom. I am terrified to think he may still be out there, searching. I am terrified to think he may have realized he has been damned to a pointless existence, a life of grasping at smoke. I am terrified to think that I have been crueler than God.

15

Scavengers

FALL BROUGHT the first big rains, making the smells more pungent and turning the leaves red. The earth was sodden and the brook had swelled; the low sun lengthened the shadows in the late afternoon. I watched as the swallows flew off in the distance, abruptly changing directions and parting ways, warbling their goodbyes. It can't be easy to live in a place for only a season, I thought. Anja learned to sleep at night and stay awake during the day. While I went about my usual tasks, she took care of the den and the cooking. I had to teach her how to do both. It had always been her mother who'd looked after the family, and after she died her sister had taken over. Anja was the youngest. But her father had been the one in charge. Everything had bent to his will. None of them had had a happy life. They could not go out, or move away, or choose for themselves. As she told me these things she clumsily cracked two eggs on a plate, struggling to follow the directions I'd given her, and with the best of intentions. Behind those beautiful eyes there was no room for anything but my image. She loved me from ears to tail, and she breathed my every breath. My past didn't faze her; like a real animal, she inhabited the present, and just then she found it the most beautiful present she could inhabit. We spent whole days together, listening to the rain fall and feeling the first cold air come in through the window. She was always at peace, safe and sound, nuzzled close to my heart. Which, every now and then, slowed its beating. I am sure this didn't escape her.

"Why did you come with your brother that day?" I asked her once.

It was evening, and we were sitting by the fire. I'd often thought it over. If she hadn't come with Hector to ask for the chickens, we never would have met. The question surprised her. Evidently, these thoughts made of *buts* and *ifs* formed only in my head. I have never met another animal with this annoying defect. It has to do with the before and the after, and with God.

She had escaped, she told me. Every now and then she managed to. She followed Hector, and her brother let her. That day they had gone to Solomon's hill.

"Have you always been crippled?" she asked me, after seeing me lost in thought for too long.

I looked at her blankly. From far away and long ago, I was beset by images of another life.

I told her that when I was small I'd climbed a tree, preying on a bird's nest. A branch had snapped and I'd fallen to the ground. I stopped talking. Anja nodded and buried her face in my chest. In my head the story continued. I stared into the fire and saw my mother, Leroy and Otis, Cara and Louise. I could still smell those first scents, and noises, and this frightened me. It was all in the past. Anja raised her head and saw me weeping.

"Are you ill?" she asked.

"No, just tired."

And she said nothing further. She went back to warming my chest, the flames blazed high before they began to die down, and like them my heart too grew quiet.

Anja was happy even when she slept.

One day she told me she was pregnant.

I happened to see a family of badgers stopping in the valley. The male was wearing a big bundle on his back. There was no question they were in search of a den. I went out to meet them, stopping a short distance away. When they saw me coming, they hid the little ones behind them, but they didn't run.

"Get out of here!" I shouted. "This is my territory!"

The male hesitated for a moment. "Who are you, cripple?" he said.

"I own this hill. Get lost!"

He burst out laughing. Then I edged closer, baring my teeth, and it was the female who spoke.

"Come on, let's go."

The badger loaded the bundle on his shoulders and shot me a dirty look.

"Watch out, cripple, winter is coming," he hissed.

And they went away. He was right, though. Fall was giving way to colder weather and the whole forest was in a hurry, beginning to feel the pinch of hunger. I, for my part, didn't remember what hunger was.

One morning I found the vineyard torn up from end to end. They had uprooted everything, carried off the vines without my even noticing. Soon after, the same thing happened to the pumpkins; they all disappeared in a night, along with the bulk of the hens. By then it was clear to me word had gotten around that Solomon was dead and that the big black dog was no longer standing guard.

My hill was falling prey to bandits and vagabonds in search of food before the snowfall. I should have seen it coming.

Solomon had never let anything go to waste. He gathered in everything before the cold weather, even though no one would have dared to steal it. He knew which day the apples would mellow and when the wheat needed to be harvested. There was nothing he didn't take into account, including the hunger pangs of others, which is why he never had Joel venture too far. I had sat there contemplating my hill and done nothing, as if nothing had changed. Perhaps that was the difference between a man and an animal; I hadn't given things any thought, and now I was paying for it.

I began to gather up the remaining vegetables, moving the chickens into my room, where we slept. I did what I could, but each morning when I woke I saw that they'd stolen from whatever I hadn't managed to bring in. They robbed our den too. Anja was anxious. Her belly had grown and she moved with difficulty, shifting between the bed and the kitchen.

"What can we do?" she said to me one evening while we were sitting at the table.

Stooped with fatigue, unable to offer her any words of comfort, I gave her a smile. That made her even more anxious. The next morning when I woke I saw her through the window. She was trudging through the pumpkin patch, turning the soil in search of whatever the bandits had left behind. She must have been out there for a while. There was a light rain falling, but she was drenched.

I ran out of the den straightaway. When she saw me she raised her head, trying to conceal her disappointment; all she had in her paws were some roots, and she gave me the same sort of smile I'd given her, as if copying me. I picked her up and carried her back to bed. She was so light, there was no risk of us falling.

"I want to be of help," she whispered.

"I'll take care of it," I replied.

"You're exhausted." She said it with great apprehension. I heaved a sigh.

She looked at me searchingly, as if to hold on to me, as if I were running away.

"Don't get into trouble, I beg you."

I began staying up all night, but no one came. During the day I couldn't sleep. I checked the windows. I looked at Anja lying on the bed. She called me, but I was slow to go to her.

Sometimes she seemed such a stranger. I asked myself what she was doing there with me, why she had chosen me, and the only answer I could think of was love. This made me happy, but I felt sorry for her.

Biko would have been better at protecting her. He'd come from wherever it was knowing how to fight, sturdy and strong. When food was scarce, he would have gone hunting. He would have put the bandits to flight. He would have vanquished the winter. With him, love would have been enough.

"Sleep tonight, get some rest."

"No, they have to know that we're here."

And I went on keeping watch from atop Joel's boulder, beneath the stars and clouds.

"Stop it, you're going to make yourself ill," she told me one evening while we were eating. She took me by the paw, tears in her eyes. "Gather the rest of what we need and don't go out there anymore."

I could hardly hear what she was saying. I stared off into a corner of the room. I was defending my things. There could be nothing more just for an animal, or a man, to do. God said so.

The next evening I could make out three bastards wandering around the apple tree, sniffing the air. My fur bristled, I got up from the table, and ignoring Anja's cries, I went outside. I saw them nosing at the ground. They had come for Solomon, and I hurled myself in their direction.

"Get off my territory!" I shouted.

They were boars, young and strong. I did not stop.

"Leave him alone, you bastards!"

The boars took a few steps backward at first, but then they made out who I was. Only then did it dawn on me that they were eating fallen apples.

"Who are you, cripple?" they asked.

"I'm Archy, and you're on my territory."

They laughed. With a leap, catching them off guard, I managed to bite the ear of the boar nearest me. He screamed and dragged me along for a few feet before slamming me on the ground. The other two charged at me together, but they jostled each other and I managed to scramble out of the way. The first came back at me from behind, trying to hurt me with his tusks. And it was at that point that Anja came down from the den, holding her belly with both paws.

"Enough! Enough!"

The boars shook themselves, saw her coming, and stopped in their tracks.

"Take what you want but don't hurt him!"

That's all she had to say. Those boars weren't bandits, and they weren't desperate. They were young enough to still have a father and a mother and a den. The first of them, with his ear all bloodied, stared at me.

"This is your lucky night, cripple," he said.

They let me go and went back to gorging themselves on the rotten apples. Anja bent over me, helped me up, and we went back inside, leaning against each other. She put me to bed. My wounds weren't serious, yet I couldn't bring myself to move; not blood but Anja's tears lay damp on my fur.

I owe my survival that night to Anja and God; even today, I wonder if they didn't make a mistake.

The next day I woke with Sasha's words ringing in my ears: "Between the two of you, you'll have a very short life." Wringing my paws, I could only think that, after all, he was right. Later, when Anja brought me something to eat, I asked her if the boars had dug up the ground, ignoring the worried look on her face.

"No, they didn't dig up the ground."

I heaved a sigh.

"Archy, why don't we get out of here?"

I closed my eyes.

"Let's find another place, we still have time. We can take some chickens with us, and some vegetables."

I was quick to lose my temper.

"What are you talking about, stupid?" I shouted. "Where do you want to go—you, pregnant, and me, a cripple? Who's going to hunt?"

"I'll take care of that," she said. "If we bring along enough food, we'll get by, no problem."

She said it hopefully, and for a second I believed her too. But Solomon was buried in that place, and that hill was mine.

"I'm not going anywhere," I said.

She was tempted to insist, and though she didn't, the color of sadness was in her eyes.

"At least stop going out there and don't get yourself killed."

I nodded, not meeting her gaze. This love match of ours was fundamentally stupid; we had mated only to die together. Anja had been a craving, a thrust back into life after Solomon had left it. I looked at her with empty eyes and hers lit up. It happened every time.

"Anja, why did you want me?" I said in a whisper.

"Because you are fragile. And delicate. Because you would never do me harm." She squeezed my paw. "And your eyes speak volumes."

I kept on looking at her as her smile broke in two. Weeping, she held me close. We wept together.

They stole everything I didn't manage to bring in; then the cold came, and that was the end of them.

16

Children

ANJA GAVE BIRTH in the snow. She was delivered of two sons and two daughters. She called them Tess, Jana, and Fedor, leaving the firstborn's name up to me. The sight of my children filled my heart and pierced it. They stumbled over the bed with their eyes squinched shut; they were so weightless they seemed made of air. When I picked them up, they gaped in blind bewilderment, which delighted Anja no end.

"They're yours," she told me. "They're your children."

I nodded, then lost myself in looking at them. I brought them up close to my nose and breathed in their fragile scent. They seemed to have sprung from nothing, like mushrooms—tiny furless bodies I could scarcely recognize as mine. They were alive and healthy, for the moment.

"Don't you love them?"

Anja adored them. She stroked their heads, now and then seeking my gaze, glancing from one to the other with the same affection.

"Of course."

The apple tree was covered with snow, and so was the ground under it. The brook had frozen and to fill our buckets I had to venture on to where the water was still moving.

The hens had stopped laying eggs, and a few had fallen ill. The vegetables we'd laid aside were almost gone. I felt God had damned me. He had rendered my every effort futile. He had destined me for suffering. I raised my head and though I didn't open my mouth, I railed against him. I never asked why. The snow continued, as did the cold, and I was doomed. When this feeling of mine was confronted with Anja's radiant gaze, I was overcome by a violent rage, and then a weighty sadness, because I was the only one who knew how things were going to end.

She was still waiting for me to give the firstborn a name. She put him between my paws and leaned against me. Together we stared at him.

"What are you going to call him, he's still no one," she said.

"No one," I said, grimly.

She gave me a pinch on the nose, whisked the kit away, and gave me a look of reproach, but she couldn't bring herself to say anything to me. Not right away.

"I like it," she murmured.

I shut myself up in total silence. I spent my days in Solomon's room, rereading his book. I ignored the bite of the cold under my fur and lit a lamp when the sky turned dark. Reliving his adventures kept me safe from winter and from destiny. I was hoping that they would shed light on something—some useful truth that would put everything in its proper place. I asked myself what the fox would have done in my situation, what I would do if I were a man. I was reading stories darker than my own, about trials overcome with wit and luck, with God on your side. I never stopped reading, but my eyes filled with freezing tears. I had shifted the bed into the kitchen, beside the fire. Anja never left it. At first she had come and called me to eat, but soon she gave up. I'd leave the room in the middle of the night, always with the book in my paw. I ate while they slept. The little ones stayed close to her belly, all huddled together, and she clutched them to her where she lay in the middle of the bed. I stared at them, and they looked dead to me, but this vision didn't startle me or send a shiver down my spine.

"Aren't you cold over there?"

"No."

"Your fur's standing on end."

I didn't respond.

"Are the words warm?"

Whenever I saw her give me a searching look, or hold out a paw to me, my heart fled far away, while my body stayed completely still and empty, offering her nothing.

One evening Anja said that she was going out hunting. I tried to stop her but she wouldn't listen; she disappeared into the trees as the sun was setting. Being a mother gave her strength, filled her with hope and determination, and I couldn't bear that. To tell the truth, I was overwhelmed by her love and incapable of defending myself. Anja was alone, and I felt faraway and small. I rekindled the fire and went back into the fox's room. After a while I heard the little ones crying, but I buried my head in the words. They didn't stop. I shut the book and got up from my chair. I would beat them; I would reduce them to silence instantly. The thought prompted my every step toward the kitchen and was still with me even when I found myself standing over them. Jana had fallen off the bed and lay curled up on the ground, crying, while the others stuck out their snouts, peering at her from the edge of the mattress. They scurried off and piped down as soon as they saw me. I watched my daughter trying to hide under the bed, and I thought back to the time Leroy had fallen. I picked her up and put her with the others, as our mother had done with him. We stood there staring at each other. We had never been alone, and they were frightened of me. I stroked them. How awkward I felt, but pretty soon I saw they'd stopped shaking.

"Enough crying," I said.

I grabbed the book from Solomon's room and came back to them, sat down in his chair. They continued to keep an eye on me, and it took them a while to fall back asleep. Before drowning myself in my reading again, I wondered what had happened to their mother, as if her absence had nothing to do with me at all.

Anja returned the next morning. In her eyes I saw sorrow and pride. She was coming home with nothing, but at least she'd tried; that was enough to let me know she was stronger than me. Her fur was roughed up and her paws stiff with chilblains, but a bright light burned inside her. Wrapped in the fox's blanket, I observed her entry. I couldn't offer her any consolation, and perhaps she didn't expect any.

"There's nothing," she said, in a broken voice.

She was a corpse. She looked like Louise.

She came up to me and leaned against my chest, and I could feel her warmth. We held each other tightly, then I let go of her. Anja still clutched me for a while, lifting her face to mine. It was as if she were looking at a shadow.

"I'm sorry," she said. And went to her children, who were hungry.

*

I killed the last hen in midwinter. The weeks that followed we spent recollecting a feeling we'd forgotten: hunger. My stomach began to take the place of my mind. I seemed to be back in my mother's bed, ready to eat my own brothers. Death no longer troubled me. I no longer felt grief or guilt for having damned my family. My family ceased to be mine. The kits were learning to talk. They called Anja "Mama." Me they called nothing at all. She suckled them, wouldn't quit, went out hunting again, and came home again with nothing.

One night while she was asleep I took No one and carried him outside with me. That is what hunger does. It reduces the world to a single need. There is no pity, or love, or even fear, pain, or shame; there is nothing apart from the blind impulse to eat and survive. The snow was coming down in thin flakes, and the wind chilled me to the bone. No one was awake. There was a spot under his left eye where the hair was very sparse. He gave me a confused look and stared helplessly at me. That little body, so like mine, weighed less than a gourd in my paws. It curled up against the cold. It tried to work out where it was, burrowing deep into the darkness of the night. Then it began to wriggle. I stood still, contemplating it, not a thought in my head.

All I felt was the emptiness in my stomach and the cold behind my ears. No one started to weep; he didn't want to be there, I was scaring him, it was dark.

I clenched my paws around him to keep him still, and I dug my claws in behind his neck to expose his throat. My breath came fast, but I was calm; everything had lost its weight and meaning.

Anja's cry roused me. I hunched down, like a thief caught in the act. She stood there, at the threshold of the den, with her fur bristling and her eyes wide. I remained frozen to the spot, my ears pinned back. No one was weeping. Anja lunged at me, tore the kit from my paws, and pressed him to her chest. Her eyes were incredulous but glistening with tears. I could see that it hurt her to look at me, twisting her face into a grimace, as if I'd hit her.

"I'm hungry."

There was nothing else I could say. Suddenly she looked lost. She'd wandered into an unfamiliar place, where everything was frightening. No one's neck was wounded, but in the dark you couldn't tell. Anja realized it when she sniffed at the paw she was using to support his head, and in that moment she came back to her senses. She turned her back on me and bolted inside. The wind howled, sweeping the whole scene away like the snow. The cold weighed on me. I had to warm up.

Anja was on the bed with the kits, beside the fire. She covered them with her body and shed no tears. When I came in she lifted her head to look at me with pain-filled eyes. She pushed her children behind her, and her breath quickened with fear. We were two shadows in the old fox's kitchen. I didn't go near her. I stood stock-still and stared at her, and she stared back at me. Anja calmed down, I could see a change come over her, and she looked at me with love. I took a step toward her and she bared her teeth.

"No closer," she said, in a broken voice.

Anja stayed where she was, right there in front of me, determined not to move. She wasn't begging me. I should have bitten her, wrestled her to the ground. I should have killed her. The truth is that the only one in the room afraid of death was me.

166

When I took another step toward her, she hit me in the face. "Get out of here! Go away!"

The kits were screaming.

I pinned her paws and clutched her tight.

"We have to eat," I said.

She bit me, and I clutched her tight again. Eventually she stopped pushing me away.

"Spring is almost here," I said. "The sun will return, and the birds, and the fruits will grow. We're so close."

Her eyes were open but she wasn't looking at me, or listening to me either. She seemed to have disappeared from between my paws.

"It's almost spring," I repeated. And that's when she made a feeble, nearly imperceptible sound.

"Yes."

I let go of her and she sat down on the bed. Tears wet her face once again. But suddenly I felt buoyant. She understood, there was nothing more to discuss; I was going to eat, and the idea of it raised my spirits. I leaned over her and stroked her head.

"I'll teach you to read the words," I said. "They tell the story of a bandit, the greatest there ever was."

As I said this a powerful shiver ran down my tail, because I really was determined to do it. I was going to share my greatest treasure, and I imagined her happy, forgetting the past. I was euphoric at the prospect of survival; that was what made me promise. I was attentive again, in the mood to talk, and I thought she might even give me a smile.

"Leave me alone," she said.

I didn't move. Hunger kept me in the room, staring at my children at the foot of the bed. Anja aimed her eyes at me. They were as empty as mine.

"Leave me alone, I beg you," she said.

This time she was the one who stroked my face, offering me a glimmer of affection. I nodded and forced myself up on my feet. I was buoyant with the feeling of having been saved. As I dragged myself out of the kitchen, I saw her take her head in her paws as if she wanted to hide from something, or someone. For a moment I imagined she was hiding from God. But she could not have known about him, and only now can I say she was hiding from her own pain. So as not to be found. Because it was overwhelming. I on the other hand remained where I was, like a real animal. I didn't care about anything except staying alive. I went into Solomon's room. I looked at the words with a calm heart, and I waited.

The next morning they were gone. They'd escaped out the window, down the snowy hill. Anja had taken the blanket from the bed. I'd been tricked. Despair—and the violent certainty that I was going to die of hunger—shook me to the depths of my soul. Their footprints became muddled beneath the branches of the trees, lost all direction, and then snow started falling. I missed them, and I ached knowing that I'd never see them again. Emotions suddenly surfaced that either I'd never felt or had forgotten. Hunger and fear made me feel these things. Because I hadn't killed them, I wanted to go back to being their father, and because I couldn't have Anja, I longed to have her again. If Anja and the kits were there in front of me, these feelings of mine would have vanished like smoke. I have no doubt about that. I wandered around the woods calling their names until I started to shiver. By the time I went back inside, the snow had obliterated every trace of them.

Anja had saved her children from me; she preferred to brave the cold and make do without a den, clinging to some hope of keeping them alive. This seemed just to me. A mother could not do otherwise. We had parted like two bandits, each going his own way.

She clutched little No one, and I embraced my misery and solitude, and from my chest there came no sound at all. The previous night we'd exchanged our last words, and I would never be able to say anything else to her, as I now wish I could. If only I'd never met her, never made her suffer, never taken her in.

17

The Lynxes

SHUT UP IN THE DEN, I survived the winter. I lay in bed by the fire, delirious with hunger. I saw the ceiling open like a blood-colored wound and, stretching out my neck, I tried to bite it. Solomon came to me in a dream. He was angry and scolded me for not destroying his book. Then Anja came to stroke my ears, whispering that everything was all right. I awoke consumed by terror. In the empty, shadowy kitchen, I waited for death. Each time I closed my eyes I thought it was the last. Even when I was awake I went on dreaming: I saw colors and heard voices, and some of them called to me. It was Louise. I never answered. I didn't want to be found. My brain was too exhausted to read, the words ran together, and I could no longer control my imagination. I threw the book against the ceiling because a crow was flying overhead; he had the fox's eyes in his beak and was waiting to tear out mine. Everything was confused, murky, frightening. I stalked the rooms in search of something that wasn't there, nosing in the corners and putting whatever I found into my mouth. At times death seemed a welcome release.

One night I heard noises. They were very faint, almost imperceptible. I went out and climbed Joel's boulder, surprising a family of mice who'd settled there and had a large litter. They defended themselves valiantly; the father bit me several times before I tore out his guts. The mother then attempted to escape, but I took off her head with one bite. Not one word was exchanged in that struggle.

I ate them all, rationing them out over five days. I tried to sleep as much as possible, like a kit, to conserve my energy. I didn't know who to thank for that unanticipatable meal: God or the mice, or my own hearing. Perhaps I didn't owe any of them anything, since the first had cursed me, the second had been stupid, and the third had merely done its duty. When I woke the snow was melting and the sun was out.

The carrots I'd planted after the trade with Sasha had just barely sprouted above the surface of the ground. They were ugly, small, and knobbly, but I picked them anyway and planted more. It was early for vegetables, but the hill was coming back to life, and last summer's seedlings lay ready and waiting. I went on without a family. I had no other purpose than to live and nothing that gave me any pleasure. There was Solomon, the hill, and me, and it was my bounden duty to look after all three.

From the moment I saw the first vagabonds, though I was still woozy from long inertia, it was clear to me that I needed to protect my territory. I spent a few days thinking it over before a creditable idea came to me. In imitation of man, remembering the time that we'd killed David's mate, I constructed the Shadow of a ferocious animal. I used wood and stones to give it shape and weight; for fur, I covered it with the feathers of the dead chickens I found in my old room, gluing them on with the mixture that Solomon had used to make sheets of paper. I made a very large Shadow, more or less in the shape of a young bear, and stuck it atop Joel's boulder for everyone to see. When I was done, I was almost frightened myself. When the wind blew through it, it seemed to breathe.

The days passed and the heat swept in; the insects awoke, the birds started to sing, no one dared to set foot beyond the tall grass, and I was as satisfied as I could be.

Until summer came, I spent my days planting seeds and harvesting vegetables and fruits. In the evenings I sat by the apple tree, in the old fox's chair, watching the sun go down. At night I was assailed by the darkness and by terrible regrets. Anja's gaunt face peered into mine, and then the children's eyes came to peer at me too. I dreamed of No one's body between my paws, as light as air. I heard Anja's cry, which frightened me but didn't shake me awake or make me shudder. I saw her hiding, with her paws over her head, but myself I didn't see. It was as if I weren't there.

It wasn't guilt I felt. More a deep distress. I thought maybe I ought to write it down and get it out of my head, the way Solomon had confessed his secrets and I had memorialized Louise. But when the sun rose I wavered. The feelings seemed so far off, and there were things to do. I had no desire to take the time to remind myself of what I'd done. Every night in my dreams, it came back to me.

I learned to appreciate solitude and found peace with God. It was clear to me that the world hates no one, and if it's cruel, that's because we ourselves are cruel. God's one error was to have wanted us to take part in things, men and animals alike. I absolved myself and made peace with those who had trespassed against me because, outside of our own heads, pain has no weight at all—because evil does not exist.

Then they showed up.

*

"Cripple!" they called.

I was climbing the hill carrying the water bucket on a clear afternoon.

"Cripple!"

At the edge of the trees was a lynx. He stood with his front paw poised in front of him, unsure whether to go on or not. He had his ears pricked and was on the alert. He shot a glance at the Shadow atop the boulder and then at me. My fur bristled, and I tingled with a rush of fear and awe.

"Get out of here!" I shouted, setting down the bucket.

"We want to talk, cripple!"

And behind him another lynx appeared, even larger, older, with awful eyes.

"I'm with my father, who is old and tired," he continued. "There are a couple of things we want to know."

"I don't know anything!" I shouted. "Go away!"

The two lynxes wavered. I saw the old one whisper to his son, who then turned his head back to look at me.

"Who's on top of that boulder, cripple?" he asked. "Is that your master?"

The Shadow loomed imposingly above my head, like a bear at rest, but at any moment ready to fly into a rage.

"I don't have masters," I replied. "And that beast does whatever I tell him to do! Now go away from here!"

They didn't budge. They stood there staring at the illusion I had created, trying to figure out what kind of animal it was. They weren't

too intelligent. The young one squinted to see it better, and the old
one spoke.

"We have journeyed a long way, cripple!" he said in a hoarse and
frightening voice. "Just to exchange a few words with you!"

I took a deep breath and summoned all my courage.

"Are you deaf? I told you to go away from here!" I shouted. "Go
away from here, or I'll have you torn limb from limb!"

The two lynxes shook themselves and swayed where they stood,
and then the younger one turned his back to leave.

"All right, cripple," said the old one, still staring at me with his
awful eyes. "We're going, we're going."

They disappeared into the trees. I stood stock-still for a spell,
waiting for them to reappear. Once the fear had passed I picked up
the bucket and went back to work.

"Cripple!"

The next morning they were back, just as before. The son stood
in front and the father behind, both shifting their gaze from me to
the top of the boulder. I'd been busy picking grapes and spun around
with a start. The young one held up a hen with her legs tied and her
wings batting above his ears. He made sure I got a good look at her.
He made sure my fakery got an eyeful too.

"Look, cripple! It's for you!"

Speechless, I stared at the chicken. I hadn't eaten meat in so long
I couldn't even remember the taste.

"She lays eggs! You can make us some chicks!" he said. "Isn't that
a coop over there?" And he pointed at the empty coop.

"Who did you steal them from?" I boomed.

The lynxes stood there dumbstruck.

"Nobody...we found them!"

They really were stupid. He addressed these words to me and to the boulder.

"Let's cut to the chase, cripple!" the old one said, making my skin crawl. "Do you want this chicken or not?"

I would have liked a hen. I could have raised some chicks and refilled the coop.

"What do you want?"

"To have a chat with you, cripple, like I said yesterday!" the old one replied.

I thought it over, grappling with my fear. It was a bad situation, and my senses were on the alert. Animals have very little to say to a stranger; usually they are out to kill him, as I knew quite well. But the reverence they showed the Shadow gave me courage. I was protected by nothing. I hesitated a while longer—long enough to try their patience.

"What'll it be, cripple?"

All right, I said. But only one of them could come up. Without a word the old lynx took the hen from the paws of his son, who slipped back into the trees.

"See?" he said. "I just want to have a chat."

And he took his first tentative steps into the meadow, keeping his eyes on the boulder. When I saw that he was getting too close I commanded him to stop.

"What is it now?" he croaked.

I didn't want him to be able to see what the animal was made of.

I told him we would talk just where we were.

"Out here? Under the sun?" he moaned. "I'm old and tired, can't we go into the shade?"

I thought it over. I told him not to move and rushed into the den; through the window I could see that he was obeying me, staring uncertainly at the boulder overhead. My heart was in my throat, and I told myself I was being stupid. I carried a table and a chair outside into the shade of the apple tree, where Solomon's chair already stood. I put the chairs at opposite ends of the patch of shade, as far apart as possible, then edged away. The old lynx came up and sat down in one of them. He was the most frightening animal I'd ever seen: his coat covered with marks and scars, his burly legs with their tattered claws, his half-open mouth that had been split on one side, giving him a permanent grin. His pale eyes were always on the move and knew neither words nor emotions. They lashed out at everything they saw. A shiver passed through me and made my ears tremble. I had a premonition, deep down inside me. Fear rooted me to the spot.

"Come on now," he said, in his awful voice. "I couldn't hurt a fly, look." And, as if it were nothing, he ripped out a filthy yellow tooth and placed it on the table. "Sit."

He smiled at me. With all the courage I could summon I took a seat at the table.

"Bravo! Well done. You see, we've come from a long way off," he began. "I dragged my son with me, otherwise I never could have done it. He thinks I'm crazy, and stupid as a stock."

His every word sounded like something breaking, and fear surged and slithered down my spine.

"I'm old and weak," he continued. "But I'm certain the trip's been worth the trouble. I can't even remember, was it winter when we set out…"

He could see the panic in my face, much as I tried to hide it.

"Tell me something, cripple…Do you have a name?"

I nodded. "Archy," I whispered. The lynx smiled at me again, as much of a smile as he could manage, and looked more frightening than ever.

"Fine, fine," he replied, "and I'm Gilles."

My heart stopped. At that very moment Gilles, the awful bandit in Solomon's gang, who had turned his companions against him, forcing him to flee, was speaking to me out of his gnarled mouth.

Solomon's description of this creature, as ruthless as he was obtuse, ran through my mind, and I retrieved from my memory of the lines of the book the old fox's fear of him and the lynx's remarkable violence. He was a botch of aberrant instincts, incapable of love, entertained by the suffering he inflicted on others. How many times had I read about him in those chaotic pages, while my master asked me to omit his name? How many times had I wondered how, if I were the leader of the gang, I would conduct myself in his presence? Now he was right there in front of me, still alive, and just as frightening as I'd imagined him when I was mooning over Solomon's stories. Gilles now seemed to grow more determined and more frenzied, as if he'd realized I was on to him. I shrank down in my chair, quieter than my breath.

"Have you been here a long time, Archy? On this hill, I mean."

I swallowed hard, summoning my strength. His face peered hungrily into mine, ready to pounce on whatever I might come out with.

"For a while."

He smiled at me again.

"Very good. Because you see, I've been looking for an old-timer like me, who has seen better days, a real scoundrel. I've been looking for him for a lifetime."

"And who is he?" I said.

"A fox called Solomon. He has something of mine, which he stole from me."

His voice was bitter. I understood that what had urged him all the way to the hill was just what the fox had written about in his book. He was looking for the treasure, the word of God, the only loot that Solomon hadn't shared with the others. Gilles was obsessed with it, and with Solomon.

It was clear to me now that Gilles had never stopped looking for Solomon. In his eyes I saw the avidity that the old fox had spoken of, the unappeasable madness that had driven him here from who knows where. Still he wasn't going to get anything from me.

"Never heard of him," I said, stone-faced.

The lynx narrowed his eyes and peered deep into mine. He knew I was lying.

"Yet I've been told that a fox lives here, and that his name is Solomon. I've slogged miles for a whole lot less. All I needed was a tale told by a wanderer about an animal who went by that name—one who makes trades."

"No one makes trades here," I said, but he pretended not to hear.

"I've never given it a second thought," he croaked. "I've followed the bread crumbs, though it hurts me to move. I've crossed valleys and mountains blindly, asking and asking, and I've ended up here." He heaved a heavy sigh, his wounded mouth still agrin. "And I have a feeling this is the place."

At that point I summoned my courage and stood up from my chair, scowling at him.

"I don't know what you're going on about, old-timer, but I've had enough. Whatever you're looking for, it isn't here!" I said.

Gilles didn't flinch. He kept on smiling at me, staring daggers at my sullen face.

"Is he here?" he said. "Are you hiding him?"

"Get out of here! I have nothing left to say to you!"

Right then, as I was shouting these words, a light breeze swayed the branches of the apple tree and blew through the body of the Shadow I'd built, which roared and moaned. The lynx pinned his ears down flat against his skull.

"Get out of here!" I said again.

Gilles got up from his chair with a slight grunt. He looked at me with hatred, yet at the same time he seemed excited, even euphoric. He tossed the hen on the table.

"Your chicken, cripple," he said, then took a few steps backward, staring at the boulder. Finally he turned his back and disappeared into the woods without a word.

My Shadow had worked, and I was sure they wouldn't take the risk of ambushing me. But they would stick around, I knew, and this worried me. I left off working for the rest of the day to recover from that incredible, out-of-time encounter. Ironically, while Gilles and I talked, everything he was looking for had been right under his paws. It struck me as funny, and it would have made Solomon laugh too: a lifetime spent in search of him, and he doesn't even notice him smack-dab under his nose. You would have to want something pretty badly for a dream or a memory to drive you through the world the way it did the lynx, I thought. But then I realized it wasn't all that unusual. I thought of Joel, of Anja, of myself.

I don't know how he managed it.

It wasn't the first time he'd shown such courage or stupidity; I'd read about what he'd been capable of in the past. To perform acts of that sort you had to be a stranger to reason, to every instinct, and to have no soul. Wretches of his breed see the whole world as their enemy. I don't know how the idea came to him. Some horrors are down to God.

I woke up in the middle of the night, my nostrils stung by a strong acrid odor. A reddish light shone through my window, and for a moment I thought it was dawn. Then I heard the noises, and the screams, and the constant rustling of the leaves. I got up and went to the window to look. All around me the forest was burning; giant tongues of fire illuminated the hillside like daylight and licked the air above the meadow. The trees swayed with leaves aflame and wood crackling and howling and crumpling up as if crushed. It was light as far as the eye could see. Overhead the sky was turning black and white-hot flakes were falling, carried on the wind.

I scrambled out of the den, shaken by coughs. Animals of every kind were running in every direction, fleeing toward a tiny gap between the flames. I spied the two lynxes. They were at the edge of the wood, taking pleasure in all that destruction. The younger one was all worked up, but Gilles stood still.

"Burn, Solomon! Burn!" he shouted. "Come on out!"

The apple tree had burst into flames almost immediately. In summer everything is just waiting to burn. Within seconds it was aglow and bending to the heat.

"Cripple! Cripple!" he shouted at me. "Tell me where he is! Get him out here!"

I ignored him. My eyes, swollen by smoke and tears, watched as the fire consumed the hill, bearing everything away. The Shadow was assailed by sparks, then by flame, and Gilles, like me, didn't miss a thing. He howled with pleasure, and sicced his son on me.

"Kill him! Kill him!"

I climbed up onto the boulder, trying to douse the figment I had made. The young lynx raced toward me, bounding among the flames with his ears pinned back, frightened but determined to obey his father. Unable to douse the feather fur, I nearly set fire to my own. The young lynx made the mistake of coming up below me, where he'd seen me clamber. He leapt at me, and I pushed the Shadow with all my strength, hurling it at him and burning myself in the process. He was hit by a wall of wood and stones and flaming feathers. He writhed and flailed, but only his head stuck out from underneath it. When his fur caught fire, his screams lengthened, erupting into roars of pain. I hopped down off the boulder. Oblivious to his dying son, foaming at the mouth, Gilles came at me. I should have fled, but I couldn't do it. I disappeared into the den.

"Where is he? Where is he?"

Gilles had gotten in. I could hear him moving near the entrance. The smoke thickened and made me cough. I caught sight of the stooped shadow of the old lynx outside the fox's room, and dark as it was, his eyes saw me escaping through the window with Solomon's book in my paws. He rushed at me with a headlong leap, overtaking me.

"The treasure!" he said. "Give me that!"

His pupils were the same color as the fire, and they pointed unswervingly at the book. He grabbed at me with one paw as I scuttled out, swiping my neck but not getting hold of me.

"Bastard!" he shouted.

I hurtled down the hill, looking back over my shoulder: impossible though it seemed, I had the feeling he would come after me. And so he did.

"Cripple! Cripple!" he shouted.

When I came to the brook I leapt in, holding the book aloft, headed downstream.

"Give me the treasure, it's mine!"

Gilles was close. Even wet as I was, the heat was atrocious, my coat tightened and tingled. The water reflected the horror: fiery splinters and burning branching rained down; trees shattered and fell in an explosion of sparks. While I was fleeing from Gilles, all the other inhabitants of the forest were blindly fleeing from the fire, passing on all sides with no place to go. The stench of burnt flesh was everywhere.

"Cripple!" the old lynx kept shouting, louder and louder.

For a moment I thought of stopping, letting him catch up with me, and giving him the book. Maybe he would spare me and put out the fire, as if it were just a whim he'd had, a prank he'd call off once he got what he wanted.

A short distance ahead, the brook dropped down into a much larger and deeper stream, beyond which the flames had already spilled over the high banks. I stopped in my tracks. The current was strong, and this side of the ravine was impossible to scale with a jump. A few desperate creatures had already attempted it, but none had reemerged to tell the tale. I went back to running along the edge of the water, still pursued by the relentless croaking of the lynx. I'd put some distance between us, but he continued to tail me, unscathed and unflagging, his tongue lolling out. Then I saw a huge poplar whose branches reached up over the top of the ravine. The poplar was on fire, but it could still be climbed, at least as long as the trunk was clear. I hadn't been up a tree since I'd been crippled, but I cast aside my fear and hurled myself onto the bark. I started to scramble up, ignoring the pain in my paw; when I nearly dropped the book, I clamped it between my teeth and kept pulling myself upward.

"Come down, you bastard!"

Gilles had caught up with me. I could hear his claws on the wood. With one paw he grabbed my tail and pulled. My cry of pain was muffled by the book.

"Get down here, you shit!"

I let myself drop and fell right on his nose. The lynx loosened his grip and slipped; I held on tight and started climbing back up.

"You're dead! You're dead!"

I reached the branch above the edge of the ravine, the stream roaring far below. Just as I was about to take the leap, the branch bent and began to sway. I paused in my rush to get nowhere, away from the void, away from the water rushing down there in the darkness. But Gilles was still there. The flames behind him illuminated his frenzied gaze and his horrible face with its permanent grin.

"Give me that treasure, you lame cripple, it belongs to me," he growled, edging toward me.

The branch bent farther. I removed the book from my mouth.

"Stop!" I said, but he continued toward me.

"Give me that!"

The branch was breaking. I heard it creak, bowing lower and lower as we swayed and swayed.

"Stop it, you stupid animal, we're going to die!"

Gilles burst out laughing. He leaned toward me and reached out his paw with ravenous eyes, delighted by my fear.

"I don't die," he said.

In his attempt to hit me he leaned too far, and the branch cracked. In the instant that preceded the crash I had time to read what was written in his eyes. I saw his life, and his bewilderment. In the air he launched himself at me, grasping for his treasure, even managing to touch it. Then we fell into the blackness of the water.

The rapids dragged me up and down. I was still holding on to the book, which made it harder to stay afloat. It took all my energy not to let go of it. I couldn't see anything and, time and again, was slammed up against rocks, then sucked under in violent somersaults. I swallowed too much water; my breath grew tainted and swelled up with death. A huge tree trunk, struggling through the waters with me, was my salvation. I hooked myself onto it with one paw and dug in my claws, but when I tried to climb on top it rolled over. I tried again, calling on God this time, gathering my whole stupid existence into that one desperate exertion, shouting out my will to live. I made it. I anchored myself firmly to the wood and kept my balance, riding out the rapids until the current calmed down. I vomited water, coughing hard. Night had returned now. I rode on, rocked by the motion of the stream, until I ran aground. I was saved, I had passed through the flames.

I gave thanks and fell asleep.

18

Klaus

THUS MY STORY on Solomon's hill came to a close. Gilles had destroyed the woods and died by drowning without finding either the fox or his treasure. Something that had dragged on for many years, for an entire lifetime, ended before my eyes. Perhaps it was already written that this was how it would be, but I am sure that God doesn't give these things any thought, that he doesn't waste his energies on the affairs of an animal. In any case, whether beaten or defeated, they were all dead now, while the mountains and the rivers were where they had always been.

As for myself, the last leg of my existence awaited me.

I woke up in a den, lying on a bed. Sunlight beat through the window, and I could hear the sound of running water in the distance. There was a very strong smell. Once I'd shaken off the torpor of sleep I was on the alert, my eyes wide open. I attempted to stand but tumbled backward, staggered by sharp pains in my legs and chest. My coat was covered with burns, scratches, and wounds. I tried to get up by holding on to the night table and fell again, knocking it over in the process. My heart pounded against the floor, urging me to run. Then I heard footsteps come toward me, slow and shuffling; I held my breath and pinned my eyes to the entrance. A porcupine's huge face poked in. After a long while he made up his mind to approach me. He stopped, prudently, a short distance away. He was enormous, and he stank to high heaven. The quills on his back vibrated slightly with each breath.

"You woke up," he said.

I didn't respond. He leaned over to pick me up, but hesitated at the last second.

"You won't bite me, will you?"

I shook my head no, and he set me back on the bed.

"Are you a doctor?" I asked him. My voice was hoarse.

"No," he said. "I don't think so."

"Where am I?"

"In my den. You've been asleep for two days."

The porcupine absented himself for a few moments and returned with some water.

"The woods burned and everyone was in turmoil. I was walking by the river when I found you. I thought you were dead."

He helped me drink and I finished the whole bowl.

"You come from over there, right?" he said. "From the fire."

I stared at him. He knew the answer already; my appearance spoke for itself.

"How did it happen?"

"I don't know."

He had curious eyes, calm but inquisitive. His whiskers jerked nervously whenever his mouth was closed.

"What do you want from me?"

"I don't know. Nothing. You weren't well, and I brought you here."

187

"So you're a doctor."

"No." He set the bowl down on the night table. "Do you have a family? A den?" he said.

Here again I responded with silence. He caught on immediately and changed the subject.

"You had something with you."

Solomon's book. I put a paw to my chest but it wasn't there. I cursed myself for not having protected it.

"Where is it?" I whimpered, in a panic.

The porcupine watched me, taking in every detail of my change of mood.

"It's in the other room."

He went out and returned with the book. He passed it to me. It was damp and battered but still intact. I opened it and saw the words hadn't faded, at least for the most part. The pages weren't stuck irreversibly together. I sobbed. Solomon's book was the only thing that remained to me from a whole lifetime of memories and dreams. The porcupine was still watching me.

"What is that?" he asked.

I had almost forgotten he was there. The question jolted me back into the room in the den.

"These are words," I whispered.

"Words?"

I sobbed again. My savior realized I wasn't going to have much more to say on the subject, at least for the moment. I clutched the book to me and lay back on the bed.

"What is your name?" he asked, at long last.

"Archy."

The porcupine picked up the bowl from the night table.

"Rest up, Archy," he said. "My name is Klaus."

Klaus was a curious creature. Whenever he brought me food and drink, he would try to get something out of me, even the most insignificant detail. He tended his garden and fetched water from the river and that was the extent of his business. He was eager to talk with anyone he met, although not many animals ventured near him; his quills scared them off. It quickly became clear to me that his solitude was not a choice and that, in his quiet, private way, he suffered from it.

He reassured me about my condition. He said that probably I'd broken a rib, maybe two, but I would recover. He ate nothing but vegetables, which he also brought me, but before long he noticed me making faces.

"Let's get some chickens," he said one day.

"Where?" I said.

"I don't know. Somewhere."

"You don't eat chickens," I replied.

"But you do."

I heaved a sigh. "Chickens won't be any use to you once I'm better," I said.

To this he didn't reply, and his look grew grave. He nodded as if I'd stated the obvious, then left me alone, taking his very strong odor with him.

At night my memories snaked through my dreams, where I was defenseless against them. In some my mind conjured Anja, and woke me. I lay there for hours wondering if she was still alive, if she had made it through. In others Solomon appeared to me and spoke, but no sound reached me. His face morphed into the face of Gilles, his craw outstretched and his paws reaching toward me as we plummeted into the void. Wheezing, I opened my eyes, every breath like a knife on account of my ribs. At that point I'd paw around for the book. It was there. It was always beside me.

Klaus tried constantly to get me talking about it, though he could tell I wasn't eager. Still, he insisted.

"How can there be words in there if you can't hear them," he said.

"You can see them," I replied.

He nodded in amazement, seeming more interested in me than in what I was saying. At times all he had to do was look at me to sense I didn't want to talk to him. As soon as he began to annoy me, he figured it out on his own and made his exit.

I didn't mean to be cruel to him. He'd saved me, and if I was still alive and breathing, I had him to thank.

One day he loaded me onto a chair and brought me outside to take the air. His den lay underneath a willow, its branches long and remarkably lush considering it was the tail end of summer. Fields of tall grass stretched out in every direction, dotted with trees; farther off lay the river. The sunshine was bright and the shade was cool. I saw the hills scarred by the fire and the skeletal black forest covering them. As I contemplated the sight, gripped by sadness, my heart thudded and skipped a beat.

"Was that where your den was?" said Klaus.

"Yes," I replied.

We looked together.

"I feel like that too," he said.

I turned to him. "Like what?"

"Desolate. Abandoned."

As he said this he went on staring at the remains of the fire.

"I've never known love or companionship. Maybe I found them and didn't realize it. Maybe I pushed them away. Yet I've been looking for them for as long as I can remember. Don't you think that's strange?"

I could see he was sadder than even I was. I didn't entirely understand what it meant to feel like a burnt forest, but I knew loneliness too, and living merely to live.

"Not at all," I replied. "You're afraid."

My words stung him, and he looked at me in earnest. I'd said the first thing that came into my head without really knowing what I was saying. Yet he took it as a weighty truth, almost as if God himself had spoken to him. Perhaps Klaus was merely waiting for someone, anyone, to show him the way, right or wrong. Or perhaps he really was afraid to exert himself, afraid of his own desires. I didn't think I cared for characters like his. They were too feeble and always trying to grab on to something. Solomon would have ignored him or killed him, of that I was sure. He sat quietly for a while, then started asking questions as usual. But by then I was back in what was left of the forest, immersed in my memories, in my Great Before. I kept my counsel.

My body healed and my strength returned. It was the beginning of fall. I thanked Klaus for all his care, picked up the book, and went out of the den.

"You want to go," he said, following timidly after me.

"Yes," I replied.

"All right. I won't hold you back." He looked as though he were about to cry. "Wait," he said.

He rushed inside so quickly his quills swayed. I could hear him shifting things around; at last he reappeared with a bundle.

"I put some food in there. You'll be needing it."

I took the sack and hung it around my neck, thanking him once more.

"Farewell, Archy."

"Farewell."

I let my paws take me where they wanted to go. I crossed fields, changed direction constantly, and leapt over narrow ditches where no water ran. I observed that the forests were growing far away, on the mountains along the horizon, but that the nearer trees were all ashen and stunted. I paused. So great was the peacefulness of my surroundings that my need to keep moving left me, made it loathsome, and laid it bare. I asked myself where I was headed and why. I was getting old. There was nowhere for me to go and nothing for me to do. Faced with the mountains in the distance, my curiosity recoiled, returning to me as docile as could be. I sat down and took a deep breath. I thought about the book. I couldn't risk losing something so important—this treasure. I had no need for more adventures. I asked myself how long I could go on protecting it, risking my hide to keep it safe. I thought about the porcupine, his den, and his gentle ways. The wind stirred the grass, making it rustle soft and slow. It caressed my heart with the same soft slowness. There was only one thing left for me to do, and even before I'd started out I'd known what it was.

Klaus's face lit up when he saw me outside his den.

"What happened to you?" he said.

"I'm going to stay, if that's all right."

The porcupine gave me a big smile and invited me in. I watched as he plucked out his quills with joy. One of them rolled against my paw, and I picked it up; it was hard and tapered, the finest pen imaginable. I hefted it for a moment. It fit perfectly in my grip. Klaus stared at me in disbelief, as if I weren't really there in front of him. I held up the book.

"Do you want me to teach you the words?" I asked him.

"You decide, Archy."

He had spoken without listening to me.

"No. It has to be something you want," was my stern reply.

Klaus shook himself, then looked at the book. I recognized the enormous curiosity emanating from his eyes.

"It is," he said.

19

The Rest of My Life

AND THUS I STOPPED HERE, in the place from which I write, and the porcupine's den became my den too. I busied myself in the garden, bartered for seeds, and planted new vegetables, fetching water from the river each morning. I even became accustomed to my friend's odor, until I almost didn't notice it anymore. Other families lived nearby, or at least not too far away, but none of them ate other animals. There were no bandits, and no vagabonds passed through. They called these places near the river Aquacalma, and I thought there could be no more fitting name. A year went by. I discovered that Klaus wasn't stupid at all. After a brief period when I doubted his capacity, I found it easy to teach him to read and write. I never mentioned God or death; I decided to spare him the great dilemmas that had afflicted me, and to let him have his animal existence. I believed this would be more pleasing to God, seeing that, in his ignorance, Klaus was already doing what he'd been created to do. Together we read Solomon's book, except for a few parts that I had the foresight to remove because they spoke about just those things he didn't need to know. Klaus grew very fond of the character called Solomon, my old master, and this fondness only increased his attachment to me, until it became a sort of blind admiration. He asked me many times whether it wasn't in fact my story under a false name, and each time I told him no, and thought back on the fox. My story was another thing altogether, and the only one who knew it was me. At certain moments I felt a growing, nearly euphoric need to tell the tale, to get it all down, for good. But I kept putting it off.

I taught Klaus how to make paper and how to bind the sheets after bathing them in a mixture that made them resilient. I showed him how to make colors that stayed fast over time and didn't fade. He was an excellent student, and I was sure he would improve with time if he kept at it. He followed me attentively and obeyed all my instructions: when he made a mistake he didn't lose his temper, and I didn't lose mine. He was well versed in the properties of herbs and garlic, and had treated his own ailments all his life. I asked him to write down what he knew about these matters, and eventually he taught me too.

At dusk I would carry my chair outside and sit staring at the burnt forest. Klaus would go and wander by the river. He knew by now that at that hour I didn't like to be pestered.

One day he came back with a cat. Who seemed to be quite fearless in my presence.

"Are you the one who draws words?" he said.

I stiffened and stared at him. Klaus looked at me with pride.

"No," I said.

The cat was confused.

"Yes you are," he insisted. "There aren't any other beech martens around here. And you live with the porcupine, yes?"

I leapt from my chair and was on top of him before he could even close his mouth. I bit his paw and struck him hard, twice, on the

195

snout. The cat screamed in pain and beat a hasty retreat, disappearing into the tall grass.

"And don't come back!" I shouted after him.

Klaus was shocked. He shrank back as I strode toward him, though he was twice my size.

"Are you stupid?" I said.

"Maybe, I don't know. What have I done?"

"Did you talk about the book?"

"Yes, I did mention it to someone."

He said this in all humility, terrified to see what my reaction would be. I raised one paw as if it to hit him, and he cowered with a stifled groan, sticking out his quills involuntarily. But I didn't hit him.

"Don't do it again," I said.

I didn't have to repeat myself. Two days later he brought me a pair of chickens, for which he'd traded a few sacks of vegetables.

"I'm sorry for what I did," he said. "They lay eggs."

I responded with a grunt, but I was very happy.

Klaus was gone for a couple of days. He took a walk and didn't come back. At first I wasn't worried. I got my usual tasks done without him and his constant presence, his endless questions, his strong odor, and this pleased me no end. Then more time passed. I began to think maybe he'd gotten lost. Before I made up my mind to go looking for him, though, he turned up. He was happy, rather woozy, and stank more than ever. But he was fine, and I didn't ask any questions. It wasn't long before he told me the story of his own volition, pursuing me from room to room. He'd met a female far away down the river. He had surprised her taking a bath and frightened her so she'd nearly drowned. He had dived in to save her, and as he pulled her out she clung to him, not letting go even once they'd reached the bank. They had dried like that, not saying a word, because love has very little to say.

"It's a beautiful story," I told him. Then I frowned, wanting to be alone.

For the rest of the day Klaus let me be, but in the evening he came looking for me; he'd prepared some food. It was a silent dinner. When we were finished, my friend gave me a heartfelt look, as cheerful as ever, but serious.

"You're my master, and that won't change," he said.

What came into my mind were Solomon's words: "Love is for the stupid."

"If you love her bring her here," I replied.

Her name was Elena and she stank like him. She took exception to me from the first, and I, for my part, did nothing to accommodate her. I found her stupid and simpleminded. I was sure that Klaus hadn't told her about my presence before her arrival, and I could understand why she wasn't happy about it. He had hoped to bring us together and not have to give up either of us. And he did everything he could to bring her around, but it was no use: she detested me. What she couldn't stand was the bond between us. She spied on us when I gave him lessons and winced at the knowing glances we exchanged. There were more than a few times when I had to hide the book, shut the door of my room, speak harsh words to her until she went away. She hated to see me eating meat and roaming freely around the den. Her suspicious eyes were always on me, and the reassurances Klaus gave her made no difference at all.

"I don't trust him," she said one night.

They were talking in bed, before they fell asleep. I could hear them from the entryway, where I was sitting, staring out the window.

"He's dangerous."

Klaus stammered that it was true I was grumpy but that I would never harm anyone. He said it in a tired voice, awash in sleep, perhaps holding her close. I imagined them like that, one beside the other, muzzle to muzzle, with their eyes shut. My heart softened for a moment. Then they morphed into Anja, in the bed by the fire, and immediately I tried to turn my thoughts to something else.

"He's dangerous. He makes you do strange things, and he's a beech marten."

Late that night Elena got up and found me at the window. She was frightened and arched her back, rattling her quills, nearly dropping the lamp that she held in her paw.

"What are you doing there?"

"I can't sleep," I replied.

She waited. My gaze went right through her, as if she were not there.

"Who are you," she asked. I noticed she wasn't looking at me with hatred, but with apprehension and fear, purely a creature of instinct.

"I am what you see," I said.

That wasn't enough. I watched as she rubbed her nose in frustration, and when she realized I had the book in my paws she got a spiteful look.

"Where do you come from, and what is that thing," she said. Her commands had no effect on me at all. They went in one ear and out the other. She was not a big black dog who could rip out my throat or an old fox who'd beat me if I disobeyed. And I hadn't been a kit for a very long time. My indifference vexed her. Elena was used to Klaus, used to making an impression with her shows of force.

"I come from a long way away, and this thing is mine."

That was how I answered her. Then I turned back toward the window, leaving her behind me. Elena stood there in silence for a while, then grunted.

"Here, in this place, nothing is yours," she whispered, careful not to be heard. She walked away. That was the last time she took an interest in me, the last time I had a chance to dispel her fears. Her eyes were now permanently tinged with hatred for me, and I went on looking right through her. Although I didn't give her words any weight, for a moment I was bitten by a very strong certainty, which made me stiffen in my chair. If she ever touched Solomon's book I would kill her. I would kill Klaus too, if it came to that.

Elena gave birth to three babies, and from that moment her mind was made up: I needed to go. She became more and more nervous and angry with Klaus, who kept trying to reconcile us. My friend was exhausted. He sighed and ceased to take any pleasure in telling me things. Every time he visited my room they fought.

"You're a father now," she shouted. "He can't take up your time."

One day, during one of our sessions, I told my student that he was free to stop whenever he wanted. Klaus gave a start, as if I'd poked him with a thorn, or as if he were guilty of some terrible offense.

"It's the right thing to do for Elena," I told him. "And for your children."

The porcupine looked at me, then at the book. "No, I don't want to stop. Teach me." His eyes glistened with tears. "Teach me."

This made me happy.

Elena confined the babies to their room and never let them out. She didn't want me to see or touch them, she said it many times. Every now and then I heard them squeaking behind the door, with their tiny voices. Otherwise they stayed very quiet, never alone, never whining from hunger.

"This is your den, you have to do something."

"Why?"

"He's crazy. He's dangerous. Don't you realize that?"

Every night Elena railed at Klaus, running him ragged. In the little silences before he answered her, I sensed how hard it was for him to go against her.

"He hasn't done anything."

"Not yet. You don't know him, you don't know who he is, you don't know where he comes from. And yet you shut yourself up in a room with him and do things."

"Yes."

I heard Elena toss and turn, shifting gently in the bed so as not to wake the children.

"What things?"

"Things."

Now it was her turn to lie there in silence. Perhaps she was studying him in the darkness, with her anxious eyes.

"You have children, Klaus. And you don't seem to have grasped that yet."

It wasn't long before their closed door began to agitate me. The squeaking of the little ones shook me, and I tried in vain to catch sight of them. I remembered my children, and the winter, and Anja—thoughts that wouldn't go away, boulders too heavy to budge. In my dreams I escaped from Solomon's den while the fire raged. Inside the little ones screamed. And No one came to the window and looked out at me. One morning I told Klaus I was too tired to give him lessons. The days began in a haze of melancholy. I sat under the willow staring at the burnt forest in the distance. In my mind the black trees were swollen with snow and the ground turned white. I saw the kits stumbling down the valley in the middle of a blizzard and marching right past me, shutting themselves up in the porcupine's room. If I was going to get my heart right again, I was going to have to see Elena's children.

I went into the room where they all lay asleep. I crept toward the bed and saw three furless bodies curled up against their mama's belly. They were very ugly and their breath came slow. My mind cycled back to Anja's eyes and our kits' fragile scent. These were not my children. I felt suddenly free from my pain, and I began to weep.

Elena awoke and let out a scream of terror. There, in the dead of night, I saw her soul rise up out of her throat.

Klaus shook himself so violently he fell out of bed with a thud. Elena grabbed the babies and almost fell over herself. She squeezed into a corner of the room.

"You bastard! Get out of here!" she shouted.

Klaus got back up in a panic, knocking over the night table. He turned around with his back arched and his quills extended. Then he saw who it was. I was standing stock-still, my face wet with tears, staring at Elena and her children.

"Archy," he said, coming back to his senses. He was afraid. "But what are you doing?"

The room resounded with screams and cries, but I paid them no attention. I turned to my friend.

"I only wanted to see them," I said.

I had to leave the den. Klaus tried to defend me, but Elena threatened to leave. She wouldn't set foot out of their room until I was gone.

Klaus took me to see a hole on the far side of the willow, a little smaller than his, where I made my home. Elena wanted me even farther away from them, but—I don't know how—he prevailed. In my new den, I enjoyed a view of the burnt forest and the hills. It was colder in there than I was used to, but at least the air didn't have the same foul odor. Klaus came to see me every evening, and I would reassure him that I was fine where I was.

"I'm sorry," he said, and his eyes glistened. "Elena doesn't understand that you're not like the others."

I started giving him lessons in reading and writing again. He seemed calmer than before, though I suspected his coming to see me continued to be a point of contention. The only thing I begged him to do was not talk about our evenings and keep quiet about the book, but that was beyond him.

Klaus was still a weak creature with both of us. He didn't have the courage to cast me out the way Elena wanted, and he didn't have the character to hide anything from her now that he was alone with her. One afternoon I found her out in front of my den.

"You're mucking up his head," she said to me.

"Maybe a mucked-up head works better than an empty one," I replied.

"I want you to stop seeing him, you have to tell him."

I didn't move a whisker. I relished the look on her face, her massive body ready to retreat at the slightest gesture.

"He can stop seeing me whenever he wants to, if he wants to," I said, and went back inside.

"You're not going to stay here forever, you cripple!" I heard her shout.

"May God strike you dead," I whispered.

Their young ones grew and began to speak. I don't remember their names. Maybe I never asked them. They'd gather not too far from my den and play near the coop, and I'd go out and shoo them away because I didn't want them frightening the hens. Elena threatened to attack me a couple of times.

To the young porcupines I was "the old cripple." I had indeed grown old. My coat had faded, my breath came heavy, and my vision failed me from time to time. I lost a tooth while I was eating, and suddenly I was assailed by fear. Death came, noiselessly, to steal my sleep in the night. It poisoned my every thought. Klaus caught me crying and became very worried; he asked repeatedly what the reason was, but he didn't need to know. I'd decided that.

"Are you in pain?" he said.

"No."

"Then what is it?"

"It's my own business."

I put an end to his evening visits. When we crossed paths in the garden, I saw him give me searching looks, holding back who knows how many words.

My head was in a daze. I'd deluded myself into thinking I had escaped from time, and here I was feeling the very desperation I'd tried so hard to evade. I saw the eyes of my dead, one after the other, filled with pain and wonder, looking straight at me—I who was still alive and still looking back at them. I was sunk in despair for days, tormented by *when*. But God didn't respond, and I longed to drop dead there and then.

As I watched my umpteenth sunset I decided that all I could do before I disappeared was tell my story.

I made a stack of my pages and bound them. I asked Klaus for one of his newest quills, a short sharp one, which fit my paw perfectly. He was all too eager to yank it out of his back. His inability to help me had thrown him into despair, and he suffered from my continuing silence. My behavior worried Elena too. She was convinced I was up to something.

I began to write my story. I stopped only to eat and sleep, and even then I was delving into my most distant memories, turning sensation into words. So I have wept, or ground my teeth in rage as I pressed down harder on the paper, or caressed it, in love with Louise or Anja, shocked by how long I've lived, still wondering how it was all going to end.

I hold the book between my paws. It weighs more than I do. I am hollow, I am a husk, I am bewildered. In the throes of old age, I've gone back through my life. Often I despair over pains I no longer feel and am saddened by things now a long way off. Other times I laugh. The world fades and retreats in my wake. Strong emotion now quickens, now makes me catch my breath. I've given up eating the chickens. I go into the coop and watch them pecking and once in a while I talk to them, the way I used to talk to Sara. In those moments I'm young again, but they are only moments, and I tell myself that I'm a fool. It's the height of spring. The insects are stirring in the grass, the tadpoles are turning into frogs. I stop to look around. I spot Klaus in the distance, staring at me, biting his tongue, waiting for me to wave him over. But I'd rather be alone. His fears are a distraction. The more I write the less oppressive my obsession with death becomes. I beat it back with every page, seeing myself reflected in the ink, in the lines that I trace. God will take my soul who knows where, he will break up my body in the earth, but my thoughts will remain right here, ageless, safe from the days and the nights. This is enough to give me peace, like the peace that Heaven gave Solomon. Perhaps it's true what he wrote, that I really am a man and will be saved. Perhaps God made me an animal to test me.

I believe in things that when I was young I found absurd. But to go back to being just an animal, the idea of that disturbs me. It fills me with despair. I don't want to disappear, really, I don't even want to think about it.

20

My Stupid Intentions

KLAUS CAME TO SEE ME in the night. He was drenched in tears. I was sitting at the table, intent on rereading a few passages, and I panicked. In the dark it took me a little while to make out who it was. Lately my eyes had been playing tricks on me.

"Are you angry with me?" he said.

"No."

He wiped his snout. "Why have you stopped talking to me? Why have you stopped teaching me?"

I closed the book and got to my feet. "There was something I needed to finish," I replied.

I didn't know how long it had been since I started writing. But the porcupine had been keeping track. He staggered up to me and clutched me to him so tightly it hurt.

"Thank you," he said. "Thank you."

He drenched my neck, and his quills swayed dangerously close to my face.

"Thank *you*, for saving me," I murmured.

He held on to me for a few moments longer, then loosened his grip. He seemed calmer.

"Elena is going away with the children, it's dangerous here," he said. "She saw a shadow in the coop. We can't have bandits coming around, enticed by the hens."

A long shiver ran down my spine. "Who was it?" I asked.

"She doesn't know. It was dark and she couldn't see very well." He sniffled, holding back a sob. "We had a quarrel, because I was coming to warn you. She left without me."

"Go to them, Klaus," I said.

The porcupine turned his head for a moment, peering out into the dark.

"I'm going to bring her back. I'll deal with defending the whole lot of us."

Klaus knew that if he was reunited with his family he would never come back. I saw his courage abandon him in an instant.

"Come with us. We're moving three fields over. We'll come back at the start of summer," he said.

I shook my head no. I didn't want to move anymore, or be the cause of more quarrels. I watched as my friend fell into despair, helplessly holding out his paw to me.

"Come with me, I beg you," he wept. "What will you do if they attack you?"

I didn't reply. I just stood there, contemplating his face. I was tired, stooped, tormented. I had a feeling I wouldn't be seeing him again for a while, and I understood the time had come for me to make sure I would not be forgotten. Perhaps our lives went their separate ways that night, perhaps we are bound to meet again. I felt it was my last chance, and I was seized by fear. I picked my book up off the table and I grabbed Solomon's book too—all the pages, with all their secrets. I stared at the old fox's story for a long time, unsure whether I wanted to part with it. I placed it on top of mine with a heavy heart. As I walked over toward Klaus, he turned to go and I had to hold him back. I put both books in his paws.

"The first you know," I said. "The other is my story."

He looked at me stunned, still sure I was going with him.

"Keep them with you always, they're a treasure. They will tell you many truths, they will cause you pain, but they won't ever deceive you about what you are, about what we are."

At that the porcupine understood. He let out a strangled moan, clutching at my coat.

"Teach them to your children, and let them learn to tell their tales to others, the way I have with you."

Klaus nodded, and then abruptly he looked into my eyes and asked me to go with him. I took pity on him, and closing my eyes as he gave me a final embrace, I could feel the pressure of my book against my chest as he drenched my coat with tears.

"I'll return," he said, then without looking back, he turned into the night.

"Farewell," I said—to him, to Solomon, and to myself.

But I couldn't get back to sleep. I took out a few sheets of paper, and I began to write.

Klaus has hidden the entrance to his den so that no one can occupy it. He has barred the windows with branches and covered them with leaves. He really thinks he is coming back next summer, as if the bandits might suddenly move on, like the seasons. Klaus and his family left me a few things in the garden; the rest they took. The silence is enormous, and it makes me nervous. It is there at dawn, and it is there in the dusk. An invisible storm is stirring in the sky and the earth has hardened, the way a back braces to receive a blow. I feel like an unwanted guest, I am slipping away, my body rebels every time I give it a thought. At night I tell God that I'm a man, on the off chance that he may have forgotten. I pass the time with my eyes wide open, still trying to take an interest in the things around me.

They're looking for me, I am more and more convinced of it. I sense them on the wind and the surface of the water when I go down to the river, in the branches of the willow caressing my head. The sun doesn't warm me, and the night doesn't bring me sleep. I stop abruptly and stand as if rooted to the spot, waiting for the sound that will betray my pursuers, quieter than a pen on paper. Whoever is looking for me knows where I am, but takes pleasure in waiting. He is death, I know, but I'm not going to stick around here and let him catch me. I want a reason to die. I weep because I'd prefer never to have found out the truth about the world.

I shake with anxiety but not with fear. To give a face to whoever's looking for me sets my nerves on edge. So does not knowing how much time I have left. I imagine Gilles outside the den, waiting there for me with his permanent grin, but Gilles is dead. Then I picture Joel, old but still strong, come back from the mountains I sent him off to. Perhaps it's the cat I hurt. It has to be someone, but God only knows who. Life still hasn't turned its back on me, though. I'd like to flee, to escape into the distance and live forever. I've packed up some provisions for the journey, along with pages to write on, but

I keep putting off my departure. I set the chickens free, but they haven't left. They're too fond of me.

"Shoo, shoo!" They fluttered around and then came back to me. The night is more and more frightening, the river speaks in sinister tones, and I feel defenseless. It's impossible to wait like this with a calm heart. My room is filled with shadows, and I keep my eyes peeled so as not to be taken by surprise. Dawn and daylight bring me no relief. They are my enemies too. If I do manage to close my eyes and drift off to sleep, my last thought is always the same, and it consoles me: I will go away as soon as I awaken, and whoever is looking for me will have to come and find me.

He has killed me. I crawled inside after he was gone, clutching at my hip to stanch the flow of blood. He tore off one of my ears and wounded one paw. He bit me beneath the heart and took a chunk of flesh. I am dying. I go and turn my eyes back to this page, slouching against the wall. Now it is my soul that is holding the pen.

No one was there, my son, waiting for me under the willow. He was a young dog with pointy ears. He was slaughtering the hens in the coop. I went out because I heard them screaming. He was very beautiful, as beautiful as Anja, with the patch under his eye, just as I pictured him. I didn't run away; we locked gazes for a long while, contemplating what time had done to us. With his eyes he told me of his hatred, he recounted his story, and his mother's story too.

He came walking toward me, not running, illuminated by a bright sun as if God himself were urging him onward, as if he walked with him and was on his side. I didn't move, I didn't react; I'd made it up to them, they forgave me. I observed the sky, more immense than my pain, and the branches of the tree, full of yellow leaves. I looked God in the face, and he looked at me, and by my lights he didn't seem cruel. Only he was so big my eyes couldn't contain him, and in no time the fear returned.

The ground stained red, my chest feels cold, I am holding my terror at bay in order to go on one moment longer. This is the last of my stupid intentions: to escape, like everyone, from the inevitable. At most Klaus will return and give my body to the earth or the river. Let me be given back to the others, like a real animal, because that is what I am, and that is what I have the heart to feel I am. Whether Otis and Solomon, Louise and Anja, are happy in some pleasant place or have disappeared into the night, the world is about to let me know. I cannot linger any longer. The last fear is coming, the one you face alone, from the beginning to the end.

BERNARDO ZANNONI was born and resides in Sarzana, Italy. He began writing *My Stupid Intentions*, his first novel, when he was twenty-one years old.

ALEX ANDRIESSE has translated several works from Italian and French. He is an associate editor at New York Review Books.